BEWARE

'I'll untie your hands,' he said. 'You can't hurt me. You can't get away from me. Don't try.'

'I won't.'

He removed the bonds. Lacey tried to lower her arms. 'What do you want?' she asked.

'I've got what I want. You. And your house.'

She touched the adhesive tape over her eyes. Her hands were slapped away. She flinched as he put a hand on her breast.

'I've always wanted you. Now I've got you. I'm gonna be your guest for a while. For a long, long while.'

The hand went away from her breast, picked at the side of her face, and ripped the tape away. Squinting against the light, she looked up.

The man was gone!

She stood up. Dizzy. She grabbed the top of the dresser for support. When her head cleared, she lunged for the doorway.

The door slammed shut. A hand clutched her shoulders and swung her around. She felt hands on both her breasts. She saw depressions the fingers made in her breasts, but not the fingers themselves.

'Get the idea?' the man asked.

By Richard Laymon published
by New English Library:

ALLHALLOWS EVE
BEASTHOUSE
NIGHT SHOW

Beware

Richard Laymon

NEW ENGLISH LIBRARY
Hodder and Stoughton

A New English Library
Original Publication, 1985

Copyright © 1985 by Richard
Laymon

First NEL Paperback Edition
July 1985

Reissued 1992

British Library CIP Data

Laymon, Richard
  Beware.
  I. Title
813'54[F]   PS3562.A95/

ISBN 0 450 05803 4

Printed and bound in Great Britain
for Hodder and Stoughton Paper-
backs, a division of Hodder and
Stoughton Ltd., Mill Road, Dunton
Green, Sevenoaks, Kent TN13 2YA
(Editorial Office: 47 Bedford
Square, London WC1B 3DP) by
Clays Ltd., St Ives plc.

Had you been rags or wood
I could have stuffed you and burned you.
But you were some bad breed of blood and bone
With arms that stretched an entire room,
Eyes without end and a heart of stone.

from 'The Bogeyman'
by R. S. Stewart

CHAPTER ONE

On the night it began, Frank and Joan Bessler left the stifling heat of their home and walked four blocks to Hoffman's Market. Frank wanted a six-pack.

'Doesn't look open,' Joan said.

'It has to be.' Frank checked his wristwatch. 'I've got nine-fifteen.'

'Why aren't the lights on?'

'Maybe she's saving on electricity,' he said. He hoped he was right, but didn't believe it. For as far back as he could remember – and he'd spent all of his twenty-nine years in Oasis – the market had remained brightly lighted until closing time.

Closing time was ten o'clock to keep an edge on the Safeway that shut at nine. When Elsie Hoffman's husband died, three years ago, there'd been talk she might sell out, or at least close down earlier. But she'd held onto the tiny market and kept it open till the usual hour.

'I do think it's closed,' Joan said as they stopped by its deserted parking lot.

The store sign was dark. The only light in the windows was a dim glow from the bulb Elsie always left on overnight.

'I can't believe it,' Frank muttered.

'She must've had a reason.'

'Maybe she changed hours on us.'

Joan waited on the sidewalk, and Frank stepped up to the wooden door. Crouching, he squinted at the window sticker. Not enough light for him to read the times.

He tried the knob.

No go.

7

He peered through the window, and saw no one. 'Damn,' he muttered. He knocked on the glass. Couldn't hurt. Maybe Elsie was in the back someplace, out of sight.

'Come on, Frank. She's closed.'

'I'm *thirsty*.' He rapped harder on the window.

'We'll go over to the Golden Oasis. I'd rather have a margarita, anyway.'

'Yeah, well, okay.'

He took a final look into the dimly-lighted store, then turned away. Behind him, the door banged and shook.

Frank jumped. Whirling around, he stared at the door, at its four glass panes.

'What was that?' Joan asked in a whisper.

'I don't know.'

'Come on, let's go.'

He backed away, staring at the windows, and decided he would have a heart attack, then and there, if a face should suddenly appear. He turned away fast before it could happen.

'Who's minding the mint?' Red asked.

Elsie sipped her whisky sour. It was sweet and tart. Nobody could make whisky sours like Red. 'I closed up a little early,' she said.

'Must get lonely in there.'

'I tell you, Red, I'm not as young as I used to be, not by a long shot, but I've still got my senses. I haven't gone mush-brained. Not yet. Wouldn't you say so?'

'You're sharp as a tack, Elsie. Always have been.'

'Now, I went through pure hell when Herb passed on. Miserable old skinflint that he was, I did love the man. But that was three years ago, come October. I've perked up pretty well, since then. Even at my worst, though – right after I lost him – I never cracked up.'

'You were solid as a rock, Elsie.' He glanced down the bar. 'Right back,' he said, and went away to serve a new customer.

Elsie sipped her drink. She looked both ways. To her

left was Beck Ramsey, his arm around the Walters girl. A pity on her, Elsie thought. Beck would bring her nothing but trouble. To her right, separated from Elsie by an empty stool, sat the newspaper gal, Lacey Allen. A pretty thing. The men say she's a cold fish, but they'll say that about any gal who won't drop her pants first time you smile at her. She always seemed pleasant enough in the store. A pity to see her sitting all alone at the bar like she didn't have a friend in the world.

'You're an educated lady.'

Lacey looked over at her. 'Me?'

'Sure. Went to Stanford and all. You're a doctor of something.'

'English lit.'

'Right. Probably one of the best educated folks in town. So you tell me something, if you don't mind my asking.'

She shrugged. 'All right. I'd be happy to try.'

'Is there such a thing as ghosts?'

'Ghosts?'

'You know. Ghosts, spirits of dead folks, haunts.'

Lacey shook her head. 'You've got me. I've never seen one. All through history, though, people have claimed they exist.' She looked away from Elsie, picked up her wine glass, and raised it to her lips. But she didn't drink. Her eyes suddenly opened wide. She gazed at Elsie, and set down her glass. 'Did *you* see one?'

'Don't know what I saw. Not sure I saw anything.'

'Mind if I . . . ?' Lacey looked at the empty stool between them.

'Help yourself.'

She slid off her stool and climbed onto the one beside Elsie.

'This is just between us. I don't want to be written up in the *Trib*, everyone in town saying Elsie's got cards gone.'

'I promise.'

'Okay then.'

A hand from behind patted her shoulder. She jumped, splashing her dress.

'Jeez, I'm sorry!'

'Lord!' She looked around. 'Frank, you scared the day-lights outa me!'

'I'm really sorry. Gosh, I . . .'

'Well, that's all right.'

'Let me get you another drink.'

'I won't argue with that.'

He nodded a greeting to Lacey, then smiled at Elsie. 'I guess I owed you a scare, though, after the one I just got at your store.'

'What do you mean?'

'Have you got a watchdog in there, or something?'

'What happened?'

'We were over at your place a few minutes ago. I looked in the door, you know, to see if you were in, and something gave it a bash you wouldn't believe. Scared the socks off me.'

'Did you see what it was?' Lacey asked.

'I didn't see anything. It sure gave me a start, though. Did you get yourself a dog, Elsie?'

'I don't keep animals. All they do is die on you.'

'What was it, then?'

'I wish I knew,' Elsie said. 'Heard something, myself, around nine. Sounded like someone walking. I looked everywhere – up and down the aisles, back in the storage room. I even checked the meat locker. No one in the store but yours truly. Then the cash register opened on its own accord, and that did it. I closed up.'

'Maybe you've got a ghost,' Frank said, half grinning.

'That's what I wonder,' Elsie said. 'What do you think, Lacey?'

'I think we should drive over to your store and take a look.'

Lacey swung her car into the parking lot of Hoffman's Market.

'Why don't you wait here,' Frank told his wife.

'And miss the fun?' She flung open a rear door, climbed out, and smiled at Lacey. 'You think we'll make the paper?'

'That depends on what's inside,' she said, and followed Elsie to the door.

'We'll make the paper for sure,' said Frank, 'if we all get slaughtered in there.'

Elsie frowned over her shoulder. 'You do talk, Frank.'

'If you're so nervous,' Joan told him, 'maybe *you* should wait in the car.'

'And let you get slaughtered without me? How would that look?'

Elsie peered through a window. 'I don't see anything. Course, I didn't before.'

'Let's go in,' Lacey whispered. She rubbed her arms. In spite of the night's heat, she had goosebumps. Maybe this wasn't such a great idea, she decided as Elsie pushed the key into the lock. But it had been *her* idea. She could hardly back out now. Besides, she did want to find out what had caused the trouble.

Elsie pushed open the door and entered. Lacey followed her in. The hardwood floor creaked under their footsteps. They stopped near the counter. Except for the light from a ceiling fixture near the door, the store was dark. Lacey could see only a short distance up the aisles.

'Maybe you could turn on some . . .'

'Holy shit!'

She swung around. Frank's hand was still on the door. He'd stopped in the midst of shutting it. He and Joan stood motionless, staring.

'I'll be . . .' said Elsie.

Lacey walked to the door and crouched. 'Wicked looking thing,' she said. The meat cleaver was buried deep in the wood only inches beneath the lower windows.

'A little higher . . .' Frank muttered.

'That's what hit the door!' Joan cried.

'That's right.'

'God, you could've been killed!'

Lacey stood up. 'I think we'd better get out of here.'

'Yeah,' Frank said. 'And quick. Whoever threw that sucker isn't fooling around.'

'Shouldn't we call the police?' Elsie asked.

'From the bar. Come on.'

Oasis Tribune

Saturday, July 12

BURGLAR ATTACKS LOCAL MAN

Frank Bessler, local T.V. repairman, narrowly escaped injury last night when he interrupted a burglary in progress at Hoffman's Market.

Bessler and his wife, Joan, arrived at the market shortly after it was closed for the night by its proprietor, Elsie Hoffman. As Bessler peered inside, the front door was shaken by a cleaver thrown by an unseen assailant.

Police were summoned after Bessler notified Mrs Hoffman of the occurrence. The responding patrolman, Ralph Lewis, searched the market and determined that the assailant had fled.

No signs of forced entry were found. According to Mrs Hoffman, no money was taken. The empty wrappers of two T-bone steaks were discovered behind the meat counter, along with an empty bottle of wine.

Elsie Hoffman, who has operated the market alone since the demise of her husband, admits she is troubled by the burglary and the assault on Bessler, but has no plans to change the store's hours of operation. 'Fear can run your life if you let it,' she states. 'I won't let it run mine.'

Says Bessler, 'I went in for a beer and almost bought a farm.'

MARKET HIT AGAIN

Hoffman's Market, over the weekend, was again the target of an unknown vandal. Opening her store for business, Monday morning, proprietor Elsie Hoffman found the empty wrappings of beef, potato chips, and other edibles scattered about the floor.

'Looks like someone had another feast,' commented Mrs Hoffman, whose store was the scene of a similar invasion on Friday night. On that occasion, local T.V. repairman Frank Bessler barely escaped serious injury when the surprised vandal hurled a meat cleaver at his head.

Police believe that both incidents are the work of the same individual. To date, nobody has seen the perpetrator. Nor is it known how he gains entry to the store.

Red Peterson, bartender at the Golden Oasis and a long-standing friend of Mrs Hoffman, has offered his German Shepherd, Rusty, to guard the market's premises. 'I'll put Rusty up against any ten hooligans, and we'll just see who takes a bite out of what,' says Red.

Mrs Hoffman has agreed to use the dog in hopes of preventing further losses.

CHAPTER TWO

DUSK SETTLED over Bayou Lafourche, and the participants began to arrive. They came in dinghies and skiffs and canoes, silently paddling or poling their way around the bend, landing on the high ground and dragging their vessels ashore.

The man's black, sweaty face looked grim in the telescopic sight of Matthew Dukane's rifle. 'Smile,' Dukane said. Though his whisper seemed loud, he doubted anyone would hear him. He was sitting astraddle a branch high in the tree. Even in total silence, those below would be unlikely to catch his whisper; in all this din, they didn't stand a chance.

A Chicago boy, Dukane didn't know what the hell was causing such a racket. The place sounded like the Brookfield Zoo gone manic. Or the jungles of Vietnam.

He sighted in an old, white crone. A teenaged girl with corn-rows. A fat white man who looked like a good ol' boy. A bony red-haired gal. A strikingly beautiful mulatto woman. A black fellow with the build of a Sumo wrestler.

Quite a congregation, Dukane thought. But then, Laveda was quite a woman. Hard to imagine anyone so beautiful could be so damned evil.

She hadn't shown herself yet. That was her style, though. Like most ladies who thought too highly of themselves, she had a fondness for dramatic entrances.

The drums began. Dukane glanced at the three drummers. They were all black men, naked to the waist, squatting at the edge of the clearing with their drums between their legs. They thumped the skins with their open hands.

Dukane looked away, and saw another skiff land. Its

14

lone occupant climbed out. A white girl in cut-offs and a T-shirt. Quite attractive. He found her in the scope. The girl was Alice Donovan, no doubt about it. Though her hair was longer now, she still bore a striking resemblance to the graduation photo given to Dukane by her parents when they hired him.

Even as she walked towards the clearing, she began to sway with the low throb of the drumbeats.

The ceremonial fire was lighted.

The drumbeats quickened, and the dancing began.

Resting the weapon across his lap, he watched. The tempo was picking up, the drummers pounding out a frenzied beat. The dancers twirled and leapt in the firelight. Several were already naked. As he watched, Alice skinned off her T-shirt. She whirled, waving it like a banner while her other hand opened her cut-offs. She didn't pull the shorts down. She danced as if forgetting them. They hung in place, at first, then slowly slipped lower and lower until they were halfway down her bare rump. They suddenly dropped. Dukane thought they might hobble the girl and trip her, but she jumped gracefully free. He turned his gaze to the mulatto woman with skin the color of tea. She was glossy with sweat, writhing as she rubbed her breasts.

Plenty of guys, Dukane thought, would pay through the nose for a show like this. He was slightly aroused, himself, but frightened. He'd heard people say fear is an aphrodisiac. Maybe it was, for them. In Dukane's experience, he'd found fear to be a great shrinker of erections.

Erections. Plenty of them down there. No coupling, though. Not yet. Nobody was even touching – not each other, anyway. They danced alone, jerking to the wild race of the drums, stroking themselves as if no one else existed.

Suddenly, the drums stopped. The dancers dropped to their knees.

A single, low voice said, 'Laveda.' Other voices joined it in a slow chant. 'Laveda, Laveda, Laveda . . .'

Dukane flinched as something dropped onto his head. It

moved in his hair, scurried down his forehead. He brushed it away. Probably a goddamn spider. The swamp was full of them.

The group kneeling around the fire continued to chant.

Out of the darkness behind the drummers stepped Laveda. Dukane had kept her under surveillance for two weeks in New Orleans hoping she would lead him to Alice – but he'd never seen her like this. He stared.

She wore a sheathed dagger at her side, suspended from a belt of gold chain. She wore a gold band on each upper arm. She wore a necklace of claws. And nothing else.

Her thick, blonde hair hung past her shoulders. Her skin glistened as if rubbed with oil. Dukane couldn't take his eyes off her. She was six-foot-one of the most stunning woman he had ever seen.

The chanting stopped as she walked among her congregation.

'The river flows,' she said.

In unison, the others chanted, 'The river is red.'

'The river flows.'

'Flows from the heart.'

'The river flows.'

'All powerful is the river.'

'Its water is the water of life,' she said.

'All powerful is he who drinks at its shore.'

'Who, among us, would be all powerful?'

'I,' answered the chorus.

Dukane spotted Alice. She looked ecstatic.

Laveda drew out her dagger. Standing near the fire, she raised it high and slowly turned in a circle. 'Who, among us, would drink at the river?'

'*I.*'

'For he who partakes of the flowing river shall inherit all powers.'

'The power of life, the power of death ... .'

'. . . shall vanquish all enemies . . .'

'The strong and the weak shall perish at his command!'

'. . . shall do what he will!'

'What thou wilt shall be the law!'

'Who shall drink at the river?'

'*I!*' they roared.

The drums rumbled. The congregation, still kneeling, swayed to the rhythm.

'The river flows!' Laveda yelled, wandering among her people. 'It flows and winds. We shall drink from its shores, this night. We shall drink its all powerful waters and take its power into ourselves. The river is endless. Its waters flow forever. Eternal power shall be ours!'

She stopped and placed her open hand on the head of the beautiful young mulatto. The woman rose to her feet.

'We shall drink at the river!'

Dukane winced as Laveda jerked the woman's head back by the hair and flicked her knife across the throat. She pressed her mouth to the spouting wound.

Two men held the convulsing mulatto from behind, and Laveda stepped back. Her face was smeared with blood. It streamed down her body.

'Drink, all of you, at the river!'

As the drums roared, the whole mob rushed forward. Including Alice. They caught the blood in their mouths and hurried off, smearing their bodies, dancing with sudden fury as if they'd all gone mad. Laveda, herself, leapt and spun like the others, her golden hair flying, flesh shimmering in the firelight, breasts slick with blood. A huge, black man fell to the ground at her feet. She dropped onto him, impaling herself. As she rode him, she took a man into her mouth.

Everywhere Dukane looked, bodies were falling upon each other, mounting and thrusting to the thunder of the drums.

Alice, on her back near the center of the group, was barely visible under the pale body of a middle-aged man.

Slinging the rifle across his back, Dukane climbed down from the tree. He propped his rifle against its trunk. He tried to ignore the lump of fear in his belly as he disrobed.

A piece of cake, he told himself.

Cakes get eaten.

Screw that analogy, he thought, and managed a smile.

When he was naked, he mussed up his hair until it hung over his eyes. Then he slipped his Buck knife from its sheath.

The things I'll do for money.

Even as he cut into his forearm, though, he knew this wasn't just for money. Now that he'd located the girl, he could think of several less hazardous ways to snatch her from the cult. But none were this daring, this exciting. None would give him the same thrill.

Gonna get myself killed one of these days.

With a trembling hand, he smeared blood over his cheeks and mouth and chin.

He stabbed his knife into the trunk of the Cypress, then made his way towards the clearing. His heart pounded with the thudding drums. His mouth was parched. Licking his lips, he tasted his own blood.

From behind a bush, he studied the fire-lit congregation. No one was standing, no one keeping watch. All were busy writhing in groups of two or more, or crawling off to join new partners.

Six feet from where he stood, two women were entwined, faces buried between wide-spread thighs. The one on top was a lean, white woman with a strawberry birthmark on her rump. Dukane crawled forward and nipped it. Her buttocks clenched and she yelped with surprise. Twisting her head around, she gazed at him with wild eyes. Dukane leered. He threw himself onto her sweaty back. Together, they rolled off to the side. She squirmed on top of him, moaning as he nibbled the side of her neck and fondled her breasts. The other woman scurried to join in. She pried apart their legs and knelt between them, her mouth going to the girl, her hand groping Dukane.

It squeezed him, massaged him, stroked him. He grew hard, his erection rising and pressing against the groin of the girl on top of him. He felt a tongue.

18

Then the woman tumbled away, sprawling as a burly black man fell upon her and rammed in.

Dukane threw himself over, rolling onto the girl who'd been on top of him. She clawed at the grass as he wedged her legs apart. Kneeling behind her, he stroked her wet opening. Then he clutched her hips and thrust into her. His quick, hard lunges soon brought her to a quaking orgasm. He withdrew, rigid and aching, concentrating to prevent his own body from finding its release. With a pat on her rump, he crawled away from the girl.

He spotted Alice. She was several yards away, on her back, her heels embedded in the rump of a fat man, pressing him down deeper. As Dukane crawled toward her, a hand darted from behind and gripped his erection. Lowering his head, he looked between his legs.

A chill swept up his spine.

Lying on her back, one hand clutching him, was Laveda. She licked her lips. Her eyes looked dull and glazed.

Maybe she's too far gone, Dukane thought, to realize I don't belong.

He started to crawl backwards as Laveda pulled him.

There are thirty others here, he told himself. At least thirty. She couldn't know them all on sight.

Could she?

No. The New Orleans group was only one of a hundred. She had followers all over the country. Several thousand. New members all the time. She couldn't possibly keep track.

Her face appeared between his legs. Lifting her head, she sucked him into her mouth. He felt her tight lips, her pressing tongue, the edges of her teeth.

If she knows, Dukane thought, she'll bite. Or ram that dagger . . .

But she didn't. Her mouth held him tightly, sucking.

At least she can't see my face, he thought.

And then he was lost in the growing ache of need. Images flashed through his mind of Laveda writhing in the firelight, her skin glossy, her firm breasts tipped with rigid nipples.

Her hands spread his buttocks. She pushed a finger in, and he burst with release. She sucked hard as he pumped inside the tight wetness of her mouth. After he was done, she continued to tug at him for a few moments.

Then her head lowered. Her eyes were shut. She licked her lips.

Dukane crawled forward. Looking back, he saw her curl onto her side and reach out for the foot of a nearby girl. The girl, astraddle an older man, freed herself from his embraces and scurried toward Laveda.

He looked for Alice, and found her in the same place, still gasping under the fat man. He hurried to them. The fat man was grunting and pumping, his rump shaking like jello.

Dukane pinched his carotid artery, felt him go rigid for a moment, then limp. He rolled the man off Alice, and took his place.

She smiled languidly. Her hands stroked his back. Her heels caressed his rump. She was hot and slick beneath him. She shivered as Dukane gnawed the side of her neck.

He pushed himself to his hands and knees. Alice clung to his neck, at first, when he started to crawl forward. Then her grip loosened. She fell to the ground and he kept crawling. Her hands trailed down his belly as he passed over her. They fondled his penis.

Dukane lowered his head to look at her. 'Ride me,' he said.

Alice made a husky laugh. Then she rolled over and climbed onto Dukane. She straddled him, thighs hugging his hips, breasts against his back, arms wrapping his chest. 'Giddyap,' she whispered.

He crawled past several squirming piles of bodies. Once, Alice reached out to squeeze a looming breast and fell from Dukane's back. She quickly remounted.

Dukane continued forward.

'My turn,' Alice whispered in his ear.

'Huh?'

'You ride me.'

Dukane dropped to his elbows. She slid forward. Dukane climbed onto her back, but kept his feet on the ground for support. With one hand, he gripped her hair. He raised her head and pointed her toward the bushes. With his other hand, he slapped her rump. She whinnied and started to move.

Dukane walked, keeping most of his weight off her back while he guided her away from the group. At the edge of the clearing, she halted. She began to chew the leaves of a nearby bush.

Hunching low, Dukane pressed himself to her back. His right arm reached under her and caressed a breast. His left hand pinched her carotid. She started to collapse. He threw her over and they rolled together under the sheltering bushes.

For a long time, Dukane lay motionless on top of the girl. He watched the crowd.

Apparently, the disappearing act had drawn no attention.

He climbed off Alice. Staying low, he dragged her deeper into the undergrowth. When they were well away from the clearing, he hoisted her over his shoulder and ran.

Oasis Tribune

Wednesday, July 16

GUARD DOG SLAIN

The dismembered body of Rusty, bartender Red Peterson's German Shepherd, was found yesterday morning inside Hoffman's Market where the dog had been left, overnight, to guard the store against recurrent vandalism and grocery thefts.

Says proprietor Elsie Hoffman, who found the slain canine, 'I'm just sick about it, just sick. We shouldn't have left that poor dog in here. I just knew he'd come to no good.' In tears, she added, 'That dog was the world to Red.'

Red Peterson, owner of the dog and bartender at the Golden Oasis, was unavailable for comment.

CHAPTER THREE

LACEY CLIMBED onto a bar stool. She tapped a cigarette out of its pack, and pressed it between her lips.

George O'Toole swiveled toward her. His ruddy, broad face crinkled with a smile, and he struck a match.

'Thank you.'

'And what'll it be you're drinking tonight?' he asked, with a lilt Lacey assumed he had picked up from Barry Fitzgerald movies.

'A little red wine.'

'A dainty drink for a dainty lady,' he said. He raised a thick, weathered hand and caught the bartender's eye.

The bartender was Will Glencoe.

'A spot of red for the lady, Will. And another Guinness for himself.' The bartender turned away. 'You did Red a fine turn, writing up your story the way you did. He was almighty ashamed of the way he carried on about Rusty. I can understand a grown man weeping over the loss of a good dog – done it myself more than once. But it's a private thing, and a man doesn't want it blatted about. You did him a fine turn.'

'He's right, there,' said Will, setting down the drinks. 'Take your average reporter, he'd have a field day. Bunch of blood-suckers, that's what they are.'

'But not our Lacey. You did yourself proud, young lady.'

She reached into her purse.

'You put that away.'

'Thank you, George.'

He paid, and Will stepped away to take an order down the bar.

'Where *is* Red tonight?' Lacey asked.

George narrowed one eye. 'Now where would *you* be, if a heartless so-and-so had done your dog that way?'

'Elsie's?'

He turned his wrist over, and peered at his watch. 'She'll be closing up in ten minutes. Red's there with his twelve gauge. He'll be camping there tonight, hoping the filthy beggar shows up again. I offered my services – two guns are twice one – but he's after doing it alone, and I can't say I blame the man.' George lifted his stein. 'To your health,' he toasted.

'And yours, George.'

He winked at her, and drank.

Lacey sipped her wine. 'What's Red planning to do, shoot the man?'

'The beggar cut down his dog, Lacey.'

'I know, I saw it.'

'And was it as bad as they say?'

'My God, George. I've never seen anything like . . .' She gagged. Tears filled her eyes.

'Now, now.' George patted her shoulder.

She wiped the tears away, and took a deep breath. 'I'm sorry.' She managed a smile. 'I don't normally go around gagging in public. Just thinking about that . . .' She did it again.

'Careful there. Say now, do you know how to tell the groom at a Kerryman's wedding?'

She shook her head.

'He's the one in the pin-striped Wellingtons.'

She wiped her eyes, and sighed.

'Feeling better, now? Have another wine, and we'll talk of other things. I've a raft of Kerryman jokes. They're sure to gladden your heart.'

'Thanks, George. I really should be going, though.'

Outside in the warm night air, she felt better. She climbed into her car and rolled down the window. Her hand paused on the ignition. She wanted to go home, take a long bath, and get to bed. But she couldn't. Maybe it was none of her business. Knowing Red's plan, though, she wouldn't feel right if she didn't at least talk to him, warn him of the possible consequences.

You don't blow a man apart with a shotgun because he killed your dog. Not unless you want a prison stretch. Even shooting an intruder, unless the man is armed, could mean more trouble than Red probably bargained for.

She started her car and drove the three blocks to Hoffman's Market. Its sign was brightly lighted; it hadn't closed yet. She pulled into the parking lot, and stopped beside Red's pickup truck. In the past, she'd rarely seen the pickup without Rusty pacing its bed, tail wagging, fur ruffled by the wind. She used to fear for the dog's safety. Suppose it leapt over the low panel as the truck sped along? Once, she'd voiced her fear to Red. 'Would *you* jump off a moving truck?' he'd asked. 'No, but I'm not a dog.' Red grinned at that. 'You can say that again.'

Lacey ran her hand along the tailgate and looked into the empty truck bed, then hurried away.

The door of the market wasn't locked. She pushed it open, and stepped inside. Nobody at the counter.

'Hello,' she called.

Swinging the door shut, she glanced at the pale gash left by the meat cleaver.

'Elsie? Red?'

She looked down a bright aisle. At the far end, just in front of the meat counter, a shotgun lay on the floor. An icy chill washed over Lacey, raising goosebumps. Even the skin of her forehead felt stiff and prickly. She rubbed it as she walked between the grocery shelves, eyes fixed on the shotgun.

The air, she noticed, had the faint but pungent odor she knew from shooting skeet with her father.

Only when she was standing over the shotgun did she lift her gaze to the meat counter and see Elsie's head wrapped in cellophane.

Lacey's mouth jerked open. Her scream came out voiceless, a quiet explosion of breath.

She dropped to a crouch, grabbed the shotgun, and pivoted. Nobody coming up behind her. She worked the pump action. It made a loud metallic *snick-snack*, and a blue shell tumbled to the floor.

Keeping her eyes averted from Elsie, she walked along the meat counter. Just ahead, a display of Diet Rite had been blasted apart. Cans lay in all directions, half of them pierced by shot. The floor was slippery with a thin layer of cola.

Beyond the display, barely hidden by the shelves of the next aisle, she found Red. He lay on his back, alive, reaching across his chest, trying to fit his severed left arm into place.

'Oh boy,' he whispered. 'Oh boy.'

'Red?'

He glanced up at Lacey, then looked back at his arm. 'Oh boy,' he mumbled.

'I'll get help,' she said. Keeping the shotgun ready, she ran for the front. Elsie, she knew, kept a phone on a shelf behind the cash register. Should she go for that, or . . .

She was tackled from behind. She hit the floor flat-out and hard. The wind burst from her lungs. She tried to push herself up, but a weight on her rump and legs held her down. Her collar jerked back, choking her. Then something struck the side of her head.

She opened her eyes and saw the ceiling. On either side were shelves of groceries: cans of soup and chili on the left, cookies and crackers on the right.

Even without moving, she knew what had been done to her. She could feel the gritty, cool wood under her bare skin. She could feel hot areas where her skin had been mauled. Her nipples burned and itched. So did her vagina. She felt stretched and battered inside. Her eyes filled with tears.

Raising her head, she looked down at herself. Her

breasts were red as if they had been wrung. She saw teethmarks on both nipples. Fingernail scratches trailed down her belly. Propping herself up with stiff arms, she felt a slow trickle inside her.

At the end of the aisle lay Red. His severed arm lay across his chest. He was motionless.

With tissues from her handbag, she cleaned herself. She wasn't afraid. She felt dirty and sick and ashamed. When she used her last tissue, she picked all of them up off the floor and stuffed them into her bag.

She started to dress, watching the door, worried that someone might enter before she could finish. Her panties were torn apart; she put them in her bag. Both straps of her bra were broken, the catches in back ripped loose. She pushed it into her bag, and stepped into her jeans. She struggled to pull them up. They encased her, snug and protective. She wished her blouse were as sturdy and tight as her jeans, but she felt bare even after putting it on.

The walk to the checkout counter seemed to take a long time. She moved slowly, carefully, feeling that the slightest jostle might shake something loose inside her body.

Finally, she reached the counter. She picked up the phone.

CHAPTER FOUR

'OKAY, LACEY. If you remember anything else, though, give me a call.'

'I will.'

Rex Barrett drew a thumb along the handlebar moustache that he'd raised since becoming chief of the Oasis Police Department. To Lacey, it made the lean lawman look like a twin of Wyatt Earp. She often suspected that he'd grown it for that reason.

'You'll be writing this up for the *Trib*?' he asked.

'Yes.'

'I'd appreciate your not mentioning specifics about the way he did Elsie.'

'Fine,' she said, leaning back against the counter. There were other specifics she planned not to mention.

'Now, if I were you, I'd drag my doctor out of bed for a quick once-over. You took some good knocks tonight and you just never know, with a head injury.'

'I'll do that,' she lied.

'I would, if I were you.'

'Is it all right if . . .?' Two men wheeled a stretcher down the aisle. One hurried ahead to open the door. She looked at the body bag. The contours of the black plastic resembled a human. Had they pieced Elsie back together?

Shutting her eyes, she tried to think about something else. Her shoulder was touched. She flinched and snapped open her eyes.

'It's okay,' Barrett said. He squeezed her shoulder.

'Sure.'

'You go on, now. See your doctor. Get a good night's sleep.'

'I will. Thanks.'

Outside, she saw the stretcher being slid into the rear of the coroner's van. She hurried past Red's pickup, and opened her car door. The ceiling light came on. As she started to climb in, goosebumps prickled her skin.

She snapped her head sideways. Nobody in the back seat.

But she couldn't see the rear floor.

Silly, she thought. Like a kid checking under the bed.

Silly or not, she had to make sure nobody was hunched out of sight behind the front seats. Planting a knee on the cushion, she grabbed the head-rest and eased herself forward. Her breast hurt as it pushed against the vinyl upholstery. She peered over the top of the seat. Nobody down there.

Of course not.

But she'd had to make sure.

She twisted around, sat down, and pulled her door shut. She locked it. With a glance to the right, she saw that the passenger door wasn't locked. Stretching across the seat, she jabbed the button down with her forefinger. She checked the rear doors. Their lock buttons looked low and snug.

She sighed. With a slick, sweaty hand, she rubbed the back of her neck. Then she pushed the key into the ignition, and started the car.

A cigarette. She wanted a cigarette. A little treat for herself, an indulgence, a comfort that didn't have to wait till she reached her home on the outskirts of town. The drink and the bath had to wait: not the cigarette.

She opened her handbag. With a glance around the parking lot to be sure no one would see, she pulled out her ruined bra and panties. She tossed them onto the passenger seat. Then she reached into the bag, looking down into its darkness, hoping to find her pack of Tareytons without touching the sodden wads of tissue. Her body jerked as she fingered a cool, slippery ball and gagged. The pack of cigarettes was beneath the mess. She pulled it out, gagging again as her hand came out wet and sticky. She rubbed her hand on her jeans.

'God,' she muttered.

Her whole body ached, as if the pressure of the spasms had burst open all her injuries. She pressed her legs together, and held her breasts gently until the pain subsided.

Then she shook out a cigarette. She held it in her lips and lit it, staring at the glowing red coils of the car's lighter. The smoke was as soothing as she'd hoped. With a sigh of satisfaction, she turned on the headlights and backed her car out of the parking space.

The coroner's van was gone. Three police cars remained, as did Red's pickup. She supposed the pickup would be towed away before morning.

The road was deserted. She turned her radio on, and listened to a country station from Tucson. Ronnie Milsap was singing 'What a Difference You Made in My Life'. When his song ended, Anne Murray came on with 'Can I Have This Dance?' Nice of them to play a couple of her favorites. The songs helped to soothe her shattered nerves.

As she reached her block, she took a final, deep drag on her cigarette. She held the smoke in, stubbed out her cigarette, and let the smoke ease out of her mouth.

From behind her came a muffled cough.

Her eyes snapped to the rearview mirror. A slice of ceiling. The back window. The empty road.

Had it been the radio?

No, the cough had come from behind. She was sure. It sounded like someone in the back seat. Impossible. She'd looked so carefully.

The muffler? A simple backfire? No.

Lacey swerved across the road, shot up her driveway, and hit the brakes. The car lurched to a stop. She shut it off. Grabbing her handbag, she threw open the door and leapt out. She slammed the door.

Fighting an urge to run, she stepped close to the rear window and peered inside. Nobody there. Of course not.

Under the car? Could a man hang on, down there? It seemed impossible. But now that the idea had entered her mind, she had to check. She dropped to her knees, planted her hands on the cool concrete, and lowered herself until she could see under the carriage. She scanned the dark space.

Nobody.

The trunk? She stood up, brushing off her hands, and stared at the trunk's sloping hood.

How could anyone get in? Pick the lock? Child's play, probably, for someone who knew how. And if he could get in, he could get out just as easily.

What if it's not even latched?

Holding her breath, Lacey stepped softly toward the rear of the car. The edges of the trunk's hood were not perfectly flush with the bordering surfaces. Slightly higher. Less than a quarter of an inch, though. Maybe that was normal.

Maybe not.

Maybe the killer, the slug who raped her, was hunched inside the trunk, holding it shut.

She lunged at the trunk, slapped both hands on its top, shoved down and threw herself forward. The car rocked under her weight. But no *clack* of the trunk's lock. She lay there, thinking. No clack. The trunk had been locked, after all. Probably. But that didn't mean the killer wasn't inside, didn't mean he couldn't get out.

He can't get out if I stay like this, she thought. But she couldn't stay that way, sprawled on the trunk with her face pressing the back window, her legs hanging off. Her belly, on the trunk's rim, took most of her weight so she could hardly breath. And the pain of lying on her injuries was almost unbearable.

She squirmed backwards until her feet found the driveway, then pushed herself off and ran for her house. She leapt onto the stoop. Sliding her key into the lock, she glanced over her shoulder. Her blue Granada stood in the driveway, looking as it should, as if nothing were wrong.

31

For an instant, Lacey questioned herself. Had she imagined the cough?

No.

He's in there. In the trunk.

She shoved open the front door, shut and bolted it behind her, and rushed across the living room. She dropped her handbag on the diningroom table. Skirting the table, she entered her bedroom and flicked on a light. She rushed to her bed. Jerked open a nightstand drawer. Took out a Smith and Wesson .38 caliber revolver.

Then she ran from the house. She started to leave the front door open in case she needed a quick escape. But the man could've already left the trunk. Not likely – Lacey had been in the house no more than half a minute. That could be time enough, though. He might be out of the trunk, hiding nearby, ready to jump her or sneak inside the house. So she closed the front door and locked it.

She stood on the Welcome mat, holding the pistol close to her belly. Its weight felt good in her hand. She felt safer than before, as if she'd been joined by a powerful trusted friend – a brother who would nail the bastard for her.

Just point and fire.

The only real danger, now, lay in being caught from behind. Like before. That's how he got me before.

Not this time.

He might be in the geraniums.

He's probably still in the trunk.

Lacey sprang from the stoop, past the geranium bushes, and raced into the center of her lawn. She spun around, pistol ready. No one.

Okay.

Still in the trunk.

She ran to her car. Standing behind it, she studied the keys in her left hand. She found the trunk key. Pistol ready, she stabbed the key into the lock and twisted it. The latch clicked.

She jumped back, and aimed. The springs groaned as the trunk began to open. The lid inched upward. Lacey stared at the dark, widening gap. Her finger was tense on the trigger. The lid gathered speed, stopped abruptly at its apex, and quivered for a moment.

In the darkness of the trunk, nothing moved.

Lacey stepped closer. She saw her spare tire, a pack of road flares, and an old towel she sometimes used for wiping the car windows. There was certainly no man in the trunk.

She sighed. She felt weary, disappointed. She'd been sure she would find the killer there.

The rapist.

The man who tore her and bit her and pumped his foul seed into her.

He would be in the trunk and Lacey would pump him full of a different kind of seed – the kind that grows death – the lead kind. He would never hurt anyone again.

'Damn,' she muttered.

Reaching up with her left hand, she slammed the trunk shut. The car rocked slightly with its impact.

She remembered her torn undergarments on the front seat. Better pick them up.

Stepping around the end of the car, she saw that the rear door jutted out an inch. Its lock button stood high.

'My God,' Lacey said. She covered her mouth, and staggered backwards.

CHAPTER FIVE

SHE REFUSED to run. Back in the market, she had run and he'd taken her down from behind. It was a mistake she would not repeat.

Cautiously, turning to check every side, she made her way to the front door. She stood against its cool wood, the handle near her hip, and reached behind her with the key. It clicked and skidded against the lockface. Finally, it slid in. She turned it. The lock tongue snapped back.

Through the bushes to her left, she saw a quick pale movement. She jerked her pistol toward it. The shape rushed clear of the bushes and appeared in the open ahead of her, just across the lawn.

A man. Cliff Woodman. Out for a run.

He glanced toward Lacey, waved, and suddenly stopped.

'That you, Lacey?'

'It's me.'

'Is that a gun?'

'Yeah.'

'Trouble?'

'I don't know.'

Lacey stepped away from the door and lowered her revolver as Cliff jogged toward her. She immediately felt better. Cliff, a gym teacher at the high school, was forty years old and an ex-marine. Tonight, in his running shoes, shorts, and a bandanna knotted around his head as a sweatband, he looked almost savage.

'What's the problem?' he asked.

'I think I've got a prowler.'

'Where?' He squinted at the bushes in front of the house.

'I don't know. I think he was in my car.'

'Your car?' Cliff strode toward it, hunched slightly, arms away from his sides like a wrestler about to do battle. Lacey hurried after him. He jerked the handle of the passenger door.

Thank God it's locked, Lacey thought, hoping he wouldn't discover her torn bra and panties.

He tugged open the back door. 'Nobody there now,' he announced, and flung the door shut. 'I'll look around the back.'

Lacey held out the revolver. 'You'd better take this.'

'Couldn't hurt.' He took it, and started up the driveway toward the rear of the house.

Lacey followed. 'I'll go with you.'

He nodded.

She hurried forward until she was beside him. 'You've got to know, Cliff,' she whispered. 'I think he's a murderer.'

'For real?'

'I just came back from Hoffman's Market. Elsie was killed there tonight. So was Red Peterson.'

Cliff's heavy brows lowered. 'Fella that offed Red's dog?'

'I guess so. I think he hid in my car when I left there.'

'Maybe he high-tailed it.'

'I don't know.'

'Well, if he's around here, we'll get him.' Cliff grinned. 'Save the tax payers the expense of a trial.'

They followed the driveway past the back of the house. Cliff stared ahead at the garage.

'It's padlocked,' Lacey said. 'The laundry room's open, though.'

'Let's have a look.'

Walking near the front of the garage, Lacey scanned her yard, the lounge chairs and barbecue, the hedge along the far side.

Cliff took her arm. He pushed her against the wall, close to the laundry room door. 'Don't move,' he whispered.

He knelt in front of her. Reaching up, he slowly turned the knob. He threw open the door and leaned forward to peer in. Then he rose to his feet. He entered the laundry room, crouching. Lacey stepped in after him.

'Do you want the light on?' she asked.

'It'd wreck our night vision.'

He went to the far end, then hurried back. Together, they cut across the yard. They walked single-file through the narrow space between the side of the house and the hedge. Then he led her to the front door.

'Any chance he got inside?'

'No, I don't . . .'

Cliff opened the front door.

'Oh no,' Lacey sighed. 'I unlocked it just as you came along.'

'I'd better have a look.'

'Yeah, please. Damn, that was stupid.'

They entered the house, and she locked the door. Cliff walked ahead of her, glancing behind furniture, lifting draperies. In the lamplight, his back was glossy. The band of his gray shorts was dark with sweat, and Lacey caught herself wondering what – if anything – he wore beneath them. She suddenly became very aware of her own nakedness inside her jeans and flimsy blouse, a body beaten, soiled by another man's filth.

She tried not to think about it.

She followed Cliff around the diningroom table, and into her bedroom. The lamp was still on, the nightstand drawer still open. She stood against the doorframe, watching him. On the far side of the bed, he dropped to his knees and lifted the coverlet. Then he got to his feet again, and came back. His eyes met Lacey's, and he smiled as if to reassure her. When he looked toward the closet, Lacey lowered her gaze. His chest was muscular, his belly flat. His shorts hung low on his hips. They fit snugly. She glimpsed his bulge, and quickly looked away, a warm thickness of revulsion in her stomach.

He opened the closet door and looked inside.

36

'So far,' he said, 'so good.'

Lacey backed out of the doorway. She followed him into the kitchen. He walked through, glancing to each side, ducking to peer under the heavy wooden table that barely fit into the breakfast nook, opening the utility closet door and shutting it again after a quick inspection. He checked the back door. Locked.

Glancing at Lacey, he shook his head.

He had, she realized, a dangerous face: deepset, dark eyes, jutting cheekbones, thin lips, a blocky jaw. A somewhat handsome face, but not a face to inspire any special feeling of tenderness.

He stepped past her, his arm brushing against her breast. She flinched away from the unwanted contact. Had he done it on purpose? Staying farther away from Cliff, she followed him around the corner and into her study. He walked past its bookshelves, checked behind an easy chair, and looked in the closet.

'I really appreciate your helping me like this,' Lacey said.

'Glad I came by when I did.'

'I guess it's just a wild-goose chase.'

'Not yet,' he said, stepping toward her. She quickly backed out of range. He went past, pulled open the linen closet door, then entered the bathroom and turned on its light. He walked past the toilet and sink. At the tub, he slid back the frosted glass door. Then he turned to Lacey and smiled. Not an open friendly smile: it was guarded and sardonic. '*Now*,' he said, 'it's a wild-goose chase.'

'Well, thanks an awful lot.'

'I'm just sorry we didn't bag him. For your peace of mind. If you'd like me to stick around for a while, I'd be happy to.'

'Thanks. I think I'll be all right.'

'Suit yourself.'

He handed the revolver to Lacey. 'If you ever have to use this, go for the torso and don't settle for one hit. Put three or four in him, but save a shot or two, just in case.'

Lacey nodded. Strange advice, she thought, but coming from Cliff it sounded perfectly natural.

'And remember I'm just three houses away, if you need me. Let me give you my number.' He wrote it on a pad by the kitchen telephone. 'If you have any trouble, give me a ring. I can get here a lot quicker than the cops.'

'All right.' She walked ahead of him to the door.

'Sure you won't feel better if I hang around for a bit?'

'I'm sure. Thanks anyway.' She opened the front door for him. 'Have a good run.'

He jumped off the stoop, and raced across the lawn.

Lacey shut the door and locked it, relieved that he was gone. Had it been intentional, touching her breast? Probably. He'd been so insistent on staying. More than likely, he'd hoped she would fall into his protective arms and . . .

Hell, he was just being a good neighbor.

She tried to push the revolver into her waistband, but the jeans were too tight. She shoved its barrel down a front pocket. It wouldn't go in past the cylinder, so she pulled it out and carried it into the kitchen and held it while she poured herself a glass of Pinot Noir. She took the revolver and wine into her study and sat at her desk.

Her back felt exposed. Turning her chair, she could see the open door. That was better, though she still felt vulnerable. She placed the revolver on her lap. With a trembling hand, she lighted a cigarette.

Then she sipped her wine and picked up the phone. She dialed.

On the other end, the phone rang twice.

'*Tribune*,' said James, the night editor.

'It's Lacey. I've got a story for you. There were two killings at Hoffman's tonight.'

'Ahhh.' He sounded disgusted. 'Okay, you want to give it to me?'

'*Tribune* reporter Lacey Allen last night discovered the mutilated body of Elsie Hoffman and fatally injured Red

Peterson when she entered Hoffman's Market shortly before closing time.'

'*You* found them?'

'Afraid so.'

'Christ!'

'Before she could summon authorities, Miss Allen was herself assaulted and rendered unconscious by an unseen assailant. Paragraph. Police, arriving on the scene, found that Red Peterson had succumbed to his injuries. A thorough search of the premises revealed that the killer had fled.'

For the next five minutes, she continued to tell her story to James and the *Tribune*'s tape recorder, filling in details, never mentioning her rape or the specifics about the killings or her suspicion that the assailant had escaped in her car, finally recapping the earlier incidents at the market. 'That about does it,' she finished. 'Except for one thing. I'd like some time to recuperate. Tell Carl I won't be in tomorrow, okay?'

'Sure thing. You all right?'

'Just beat up a little. I'll be in Friday.'

'Fine. Great work, Lacey.'

'Just happened to be at the right place at the right time.'

'I detect a note of irony.'

'Only a note?'

'Take care of yourself, kid.'

'I will. Night, James.'

'See ya.'

She hung up. With the revolver and empty wine glass, she returned to the kitchen for a refill. Then she went into the bathroom. She shut the door and thumbed down its lock button. A feeble measure. Any pointed instrument turned in the keyhole, she knew, would pop open the lock. But the little precaution was better than none at all.

She set her pistol and glass on the floor beside the tub, and started the water running. When it felt hot enough, she stoppered the drain.

She turned to the medicine cabinet mirror. The face

39

looking back at her was a bad copy of the one she was used to: slack and pallid, dark under the eyes, the eyes themselves wide and vacant. Turning her head, she fingered back the hair draping her right temple and studied the patch of swollen, red-blue skin. The ear, too, was slightly puffed and discolored.

'A shadow of her former self,' she muttered. It brought a slight smile. Part of the strangeness left her eyes.

She took off her blouse. Then she unfastened her jeans, tugged them down, and kicked them off. She tossed the blouse and jeans into the hamper.

She looked down at herself. Fingers had left red-blue impressions on both her breasts.

Must've grabbed them and squeezed.

The teeth indentations had disappeared, but her nipples were purple. She touched one and winced.

Her body was seamed with fingernail scratches: her shoulders and upper arms, her sides, her belly, her thighs. At least he hadn't raked her breasts, and none of the scratches would show when she was clothed – the silver lining.

She tested the water with a foot. Hot, but not burning. She climbed in and slowly lowered herself, clenching rigid with pain as the water seared the raw lips of her vagina. The pain faded, and she let herself down the rest of the way. She gritted her teeth as the water scorched her torn thighs. But that pain soon faded, like the other. She took a deep breath. Leaning forward, she turned off the faucet.

The house was silent except for the slow plop of water drops near her feet.

Bracing herself against the shock, she splashed water onto her scratches. At first, it felt like lava running down her open flesh. Then it wasn't so bad. After a sip of wine, she lathered herself with soap and rinsed.

She picked up her wine glass again, and lay back. Head propped against the rear of the tub, she sipped the wine. It felt warm and good going down. Holding the glass in one hand, she reached down with the other, down through the hot water between her open legs. Tenderly, she fingered herself.

He must've chewed her there, too.

Filthy bastard!

At least he didn't kill me – another silver lining?

Fuck the silver linings.

Lacey blinked tears away, and reached for the bar of soap. She rubbed herself gently.

And the bathroom lights went out.

She threw herself against the side of the tub. She clawed the rug, trying to find the revolver.

Where *was* it?

Then she touched its cool steel. She picked it up by the barrel, found its handle, and gripped it tight.

She stood up. She lifted one foot out of the water and stepped over the tub's wall. With that foot firm on the rug, she leaned out. In the vague light from the window, she searched the bathroom. She saw no one. The door appeared to be shut.

Must be shut. Still locked. I'd have heard the button pop . . .

Okay, maybe the bulbs in the fixture blew. *Three* bulbs? Fat chance. How about a general power failure? Sure thing. No, it had to be the fuse box.

He's in the house!

Slowly, she raised her other foot out of the water. She stepped clear of the tub and stood aiming at the door.

Naked and wet, she felt more vulnerable than ever before in her life. She backed up, and knelt beside the hamper. Switching the pistol to her left hand, she reached in. She pulled out her jeans, her blouse.

The blouse was easy. She got it on without letting go of the gun. But she needed two hands for the jeans. She set the pistol on the counter by the sink, within easy reach.

Stupid, she thought as she fumbled with her pants. This is just the moment he'll choose to bust the door in. But she heard nothing. Only a car speeding along, somewhere far away. If he'd just hold off for a few seconds, she would

41

be dressed and ready for him. She had to be dressed.

She was bent over, balanced on one leg, her other foot high and pushing into the jeans, when she felt fingers clutch her ankle and jerk it out from under her.

She hit the floor.

Rough hands jerked her pants off. She tried to scramble up, but the weight of a man drove her against the floor, forced her legs apart. Her blouse was ripped off her back. Then he was lying on her, pinning her arms to the floor. She felt his hardness against her rump.

'Scream, cunt, and I'll rip off your head.'

She pressed her face to the rug. She cried, she whimpered with pain, she bit her lips until she tasted their blood, but she didn't scream. At some point, with the man grunting and thrusting in the darkness above her, Lacey passed out.

CHAPTER SIX

Dukane landed his Cessna Bonanza, that night, at Santa Monica airport. He stepped into the passenger cabin.

Alice smiled at him. 'Hello, dead man.'

'Pleasant flight?' he asked.

'Very nice. I spent it thinking about what they'll do to you.'

'Nothing too drastic, I hope.' He bent down and unlocked the cuffs chaining her left wrist to the seat's armrest.

'You messed with Laveda, man. You're good as dead.'

'*Better* than dead, at the moment.'

'Sure, joke. You'll be laughing outa the other side of your face when they catch up with you. And they will. And I'll be with 'em, you can count on it. I'll be the one with the knife, cutting out your eyes.'

'Such talk,' he said.

'You can't hide from us. We're everywhere. We know all. We're all powerful.'

'Yep. Okay, stand up.' He backed away. Alice stepped into the aisle. She looked good in the yellow sundress – fresh, and even younger than her nineteen years. Dukane had bought it at a Penny's in Houma, leaving Alice drugged in the passenger seat of his rented car. After buying the dress, he drove to a deserted stretch of road. He braced her against the side of the car, stripped off the oversized shirt he'd earlier used to clothe her, and wrestled her limp body into the dress.

'Are we getting outa this plane, or you just gonna stare at me all night?'

'We need to make a decision. I can either take you out of here handcuffed, as a prisoner, or you can agree to

43

cooperate and we'll go to my car like friends. Which do you prefer?'

'You don't need the cuffs.'

'If you try to get away, you'll be hurt.'

'I know, I know. You proved that back in the bayou, didn't you? Well, I'll tell you something. I don't have to get away from you. They'll come for me. Wherever you take me, they'll come. I don't have to lift a finger – just wait and use my powers to call them.'

'Fancy car,' Alice said as Dukane climbed into the Jaguar beside her. 'Kidnapping must pay good.'

'Yep.' The car grumbled to life.

'How much did my folks pay you?'

'Enough.'

'Enough to die for?'

'That's not in my plans.'

'It's in mine. They'll have to die, too. Can't go messing with Laveda.'

'You're a sweetheart,' Dukane said. He backed out of the parking space, and headed for the exit.

'Wouldn't want to be in your shoes, man.'

'I know. You're all powerful. You've drunk at the river.'

'Fuckin' right.'

'Imagine. All that from drinking a gal's blood.'

'The blood is the life.'

'Where've I heard that before,' he said, and switched the radio on. He turned left onto Ocean Park Blvd.

'This isn't the way home.'

'I'm not taking you home. You've got a date with a certain Dr T. R. Miles. He specializes in deprogramming screwed up kids.'

'Deprogramming?' She made a quiet, nasal laugh. 'What do you think I am, a Moonie?'

'I didn't hire him, your parents did. Far as I'm concerned, you and the rest of Laveda's gang ought to be burnt at the stake.'

Her head jerked towards him.

'That's how the old-timers dealt with witches, I believe.'

'We're not witches,' she muttered.

'Near enough. Laveda's got her own set of rules and rituals, but it boils down to the same thing – you're a bunch of homicidal lunatics on a power trip. You need to be stopped.'

'We can't be stopped,' she said, but the earlier tone of scornful confidence was gone from her voice. 'We're everywhere.'

'Put the torch to Laveda, and the whole gang would fall apart.'

'Shut up.'

A layer of fog hung over the road as they neared the ocean. It swirled in the headlights, rolled off the windshield. Dukane slowed down. He squinted ahead, searching for the dim glow of traffic lights.

In the silence, he thought about Alice's bluster falling away at the mention of fire. She seemed to have an exaggerated fear of burning.

He'd noted the same dread in the man named Walter. The muscular fellow had acted brazen, at first, during Dukane's interrogation three nights before the bayou gathering. Like Alice, he'd claimed to be invulnerable. He'd refused to talk. But he broke down, whimpering and pleading, when Dukane doused him with gasoline. In short order, he told about Laveda's group, its structure and purposes, the extent of its membership, the time and location of the meeting. What Dukane learned had scared the hell out of him, but it gave him all he needed to know in his search for Alice.

At the blur of a red light just ahead, Dukane eased down on the brake. He hit the arm of the turn signal, hoping this was Main, and turned left when the light changed. He drove slowly, gazing into the fog, seeking a landmark. When he saw the Boulangerie, off to the right, he knew where he was. He continued down Main, glimpsed a cluster of vague figures at the entrance to the Oar House, and kept going until he reached the traffic signal at Rose. A pair of dim lights appeared ahead. He waited for the car to pass, then turned left and parked at the curb.

'Let's go,' he said.

They climbed from the car. Alice followed him up the street, hunched slightly and moving fast, her bare arms crossed against her breasts.

'We're almost there,' Dukane told her, his chin shaking. He clenched his teeth, then made a conscious effort to relax his muscles and stop the shivering. Alice, he knew, must be freezing in her thin sundress. He put an arm across her shoulders, but she whirled away.

'Don't touch me,' she said.

'Just trying to help.'

'I can live without it.'

They crossed a dark street, and hurried up the sidewalk. 'This is it,' he said, nodding toward the lighted porch of a small, wood-frame house. He opened the gate. They rushed up a narrow walkway. Dukane took the porch stairs two at a time, and rang the doorbell.

Alice waited beside him, legs tight together, arms hugging herself, teeth chattering.

The door was opened as far as the guard chain allowed. A black-haired, attractive woman studied them through her wire-rimmed glasses.

'We're here to see Dr Miles,' Dukane said.

'Yes?'

'I'm Dukane.'

The woman nodded. She shut the door briefly, then swung it open. 'Please come in.'

They stepped into the warm house. The woman shut the door, took a sip of coffee from her Snoopy mug, and turned to them. 'You must be Alice,' she said.

Alice curled her nose.

'You both look chilled to the bone. Let's go in by the fire, and I'll get you some coffee.'

They followed her into the living room. It was wood paneled and cozy, with the feel of a summer cottage. Alice crossed toward the fireplace. She stopped two yards from its screen, and held out her hands.

'Cream or sugar?'

Alice didn't respond.

'I'll take mine black,' Dukane said.

'Back in a jiff,' the woman said, and left.

Dukane stepped past Alice. He stood close to the fire, feeling its heat through his trouser legs, then crouching to warm his upper body and face. He turned around, still squatting, and smiled up at Alice. 'Nothing like a nice, crackling fire.'

'Get fucked.'

The woman came back, carrying a coffee mug in each hand. Dukane noticed the way her breasts jiggled slightly under the cashmere of her white turtle-neck. Below the hem of her tweed skirt, her calves looked trim and well defined. Probably, Dukane thought, she jogs on the beach – just like half the other residents of Venice.

He stood, and accepted a hot mug. This one came from the Hearst Castle gift shop. She held out a Big Apple mug to Alice.

Alice swatted it from her hand. The mug flipped away, exploding coffee, and bounced off the rug.

The woman slapped her face.

Alice leaped at her, snarling, hands out like claws. As Dukane set his mug on the mantle, he saw that the woman needed no help. She grabbed Alice's right arm, jerked it toward her, and swiveled around. Her rump caught Alice low. The girl flew over her back and hit the floor with a grunt.

'Sorry about that, but I won't allow intemperate behavior.' Her sweater had pulled up, revealing lightly tanned skin above her belt. She adjusted her sweater, and stared down at Alice. 'Is that understood?'

Alice gazed at the ceiling. 'You're gonna die.'

'Not before I've straightened you out.'

'You're Dr Miles?' Dukane asked.

Her smile caught him off-guard; he'd expected a condescending smirk. 'Don't be embarrassed,' she said. 'A doctor with a name like Teri Miles is begging for erroneous assumptions of gender. You thought I was the good doctor's receptionist?'

'Or wife. I was starting to envy him.'

She smiled, and surprised him again – this time by blushing.

Dukane took a sip of hot coffee. 'I see you can handle yourself well.'

'One has to, in this line of work. I've had patients a lot rougher than Alice.'

'She seems to think she'll get away in short order.'

'I have a locked room for her, grates on the windows. So far, I haven't lost anyone.'

'She thinks she'll have help.'

'You made sure you weren't followed?'

'In that fog, it would've taken Rudolph to follow us.'

Dr Miles grinned. 'Any red noses in the rear-view mirror?'

'Not a one.'

'We should be all right, then. Nobody knows where she is except you and her parents.'

'*They'll* know,' Alice said from the floor.

'She thinks they'll find her through telepathy.'

'I'd say that's remote.'

'Hope so,' Dukane said. 'Laveda's gang believes in all sorts of hogwash, but if they have any special power, I haven't seen it in action. I observed one of their meetings, infiltrated it, even had contact with Laveda herself. If she's some kind of mind-reader, I think she would've known I didn't belong. She acted as if I were just another member of the group. They all did. So I think their magic is a lot of talk, not much else. It's a dangerous bunch, though. They *think* they've got a handle on magical powers, so they act as if they do. They're basically fearless, think they're invulnerable.'

'We are,' Alice said. She sat up, crossed her legs, and looked up at them, smirking.

'They do fear burning.'

'Fire,' said Dr Miles, 'has traditionally been associated with purification. I've dealt with satanists who actually exhibit a phobic response to it.'

'There's something else I should tell you. They practice human sacrifice. I saw a young woman murdered at their meeting. The others drank her blood. Even Alice, here.'

Dr Miles stiffened slightly.

'So it's a blood-thirsty group.'

'You could be in a great deal of danger if they do find out, somehow, that Alice is here.'

'Well . . .'

'It might be wise for me to stick around.'

'I'm sure that won't be necessary.'

'I'd feel easier about it.'

'I don't think you realize – the process could take weeks, depending on the depth of her conditioning. Besides, I really don't imagine there's much cause for concern. Her location's secret. As for telepathy, I agree with you that it's hogwash. I've been involved with these matters for several years, and haven't lost a patient yet.'

'All right,' Dukane said. He felt a bit rebuffed, and realized his offer had been motivated by more than simple concern for her safety. He was attracted to her, wanted to spend more time in her presence. 'Well, I'll check in occasionally.'

'Better that you don't. We wouldn't want to compromise her location.'

'Whatever you say. But be careful, all right?'

'I always am.'

'For all the good it'll do,' said Alice.

CHAPTER SEVEN

LACEY WOKE up, and wished she hadn't. She lay on her back, eyes shut. Her arms, stretched overhead, were numb. Moving slightly, she felt a sheet beneath her. She wasn't covered: a mild breeze stirred against her skin, probably from the window above her bed.

She tried to lower her arms, but a tightness around the wrists held them in place. They were tied.

She moved her feet. They, at least, were free.

She licked her lips. No gag.

But she was blindfolded. She could feel it. She tried to open her eyes, but couldn't raise the lids. From the sticky stiffness against them, she guessed they were taped shut.

Lying motionless, she listened. The only sound in the bedroom was the hum of her electric clock. Through the open window came sounds of birds, a car door banging shut, a power mower somewhere in the distance.

So it's morning.

And I told James I wouldn't be coming in. Neat play. Somebody'd come by to check on me, if I hadn't told him that.

Just as well. This maniac would only kill him.

If he's here!

Lacey realized, with a dizzying sense of relief, that he might very well have departed – tied her up, took her car, and headed for distant places. Why not?

Because, as David Horowitz always says, if it sounds too good to be true, it usually is.

He's still here. Probably watching me right this second. Does he know I'm awake?

Lacey tried to breathe slowly and deeply, feigning sleep.

What does he want? she wondered. Why the hell hasn't he killed me like he did the others? Don't worry, he probably will.

Unless I get him first.

Fat chance.

You can't kill a man you never see.

She hadn't spotted him in the car, though he'd been in the back seat on her way home from Hoffman's. She and Cliff had missed him when they searched the house – unless he sneaked in later.

But how, in God's name, did he get into the bathroom? That door never opened, she was almost positive. And he sure didn't climb in through the window. He was just suddenly there. A magician, a regular Houdini.

How do you kill a guy like that?

Easy, you don't.

But maybe he is gone.

No, he's here. Still here.

But why?

Because he *likes* you.

Scream, cunt, and I'll rip off your head. Sure he likes me.

The doorbell rang.

Footsteps raced toward her.

She opened her mouth to yell, and a hand slapped across it.

'Don't make a sound,' whispered the low, scratchy voice from last night.

The bell rang again, loud in the silent house. Who was there? James or Carl coming by to check on her, after all? Cliff? It rang again. She kicked her legs high, twisting to swing them off the bed, but an arm hooked them behind the knees and stopped them. She bucked and writhed. The powerful arm pressed, curling her back, raising her rump off the bed, forcing her legs down until her knees mashed her breasts.

She shook her head, tried to bite the hand. But it stayed

tight on her mouth. Her teeth couldn't find flesh to bite, only scraping it without doing damage.

Mouth covered, compressed as she was, she couldn't bring in enough air through her nostrils. She stopped struggling and tried to breathe. Her lungs burned.

The doorbell rang again.

Go away!

She sucked air in through her nostrils, but couldn't draw it in deeply enough, couldn't seem to get it to her lungs. She felt as if she were drowning. The man seemed to realize this, and pressed his hand slightly upward to block her nose.

No!

A roar filled her head. She sucked against the hand. No air came through. She kicked, but the man pressed her knees harder against her chest. Her heart thundered as if it might explode.

Then the arm stopped pushing at her legs. As she lowered them, the hand left her mouth. She gulped in air.

'I oughta kill you,' the man whispered.

Lacey kept gasping.

He shoved her legs apart, and she felt his mouth. Then he was on top of her, pushing inside her, ramming. Lacey didn't struggle. She lay still, trying to catch her breath, trying not to think, to build a wall in her head that she could hide behind, away from the pain and filth and terror.

'I'll untie your hands,' he said when he was finally through.

Lacey nodded.

'You can't hurt me. You can't get away from me. Don't try.'

'I won't.'

He removed the bonds. Lacey tried to lower her arms. At first, they wouldn't move. They burned and tingled as feeling slowly returned to them. At last, she was able to bring them down. She rubbed the deep indentations on her wrists.

'What do you want?' she asked.

He made a nasty laugh. 'I've got what I want. You. And your house.'

Reaching to her face, she touched the adhesive tape over her eyes. Her hands were slapped away.

'Leave it.'

'Who are you?'

'If I told you that, you'd know.'

What kind of answer was that? 'Do I know you?' she asked.

'Damn right.'

'What did I do? Did I *do* something to you?'

'It's what you didn't do. But we've taken care of that, haven't we?' Lacey flinched as he put a hand on her breast. She didn't try to remove it, didn't dare. 'I've always wanted you. Now I've got you. Want to know what's next?'

She nodded.

'I'm gonna be your guest for a while. For a long, long while. This is a lot better than the market. The market stinks. No bed, no pussy to curl up with. This is just what I want, and I'm gonna stay.'

'Are you . . . hiding out?'

'Oh yes. And they're a sharp pack of bastards. They'll come looking. Might even check here, but we're too smart for 'em. Lacey's gonna answer the phone, Lacey's gonna answer the door, Lacey's even gonna go to work after today, just like everything's normal. But she won't let no one in, and she won't tell our little secret, and she won't try to run away. 'Cause if she does, I'll do horrible disgusting things to her.'

She couldn't believe it! He would actually let her leave the house? 'All right,' she said.

'I know what you're thinking. You're thinking, soon as I let you free, you'll run off to the cops. If the cops don't get me, you'll leave town. Either way, you'll be safe from me. But you're wrong. Wrong wrong wrong. You can't escape.'

The hand went away from her breast, picked at the side of her face, and ripped the tape away. It came off with a sound like tearing cloth, stinging her skin, uprooting brows and lashes. Lacey clutched her eyes until the pain subsided. Then she lowered her hands. She opened her eyes. Squinting against the light, she looked up. Then to the sides.

The man was gone!

She bolted upright, and studied the sunlit room. He was not there! She swung her legs off the bed, knocking the wadded tape to the floor, and stood up. Dizzy. She grabbed the top of the dresser for support. When her head cleared, she lunged for the doorway.

The door slammed shut. She rushed against it, grabbed the knob.

A hand clutched her shoulders and swung her around. Nobody there.

She felt hands on both her breasts. They squeezed. She saw depressions the fingers made in her flesh, but not the fingers themselves.

'Get the idea?' the man asked.

'Oh my God,' Lacey muttered. 'You're invisible!'

'Fuckin' right.'

Reaching to her breasts, she touched his hands. Their surface stopped her fingers like a layer of hard air – but air with the texture of skin. She shook her head. 'How?'

'A little miracle.'

'No, really,' she said, trying to sound eager, as if suddenly overcome with curiosity. She touched his hairy wrists, his thick, heavily muscled forearms: he was standing directly in front of her. 'Who did it to you? How?'

'If I told you that, you'd know.'

'I want to know.'

'Then you'd . . .'

Lacey clenched his forearms and kicked, shooting her leg up high through the space in front of her. Her instep smacked flesh. The man's arms jerked away and he bellowed. Lacey tugged open the door. She dashed out and across the dining room to her kitchen. Grabbing the knob of the back door, she hesitated. What use to run away?

54

How do you hide from an invisible man? You don't. Sooner or later, he'd get her.

She slid a carving knife out of its rack, and dashed toward the breakfast nook. She rushed alongside the table, swinging a chair out behind her to block the narrow passage. Spinning around, she shoved the other chair out. Now she stood behind the table, both sides blocked, knife in front of her, ready.

Almost ready.

She opened a cupboard behind her. She lifted out a heavy bag. Clamping the knife in her teeth, she unrolled its top.

With a skidding rumble, the table scooted toward her. She lurched backwards. The edge of the counter caught her rump. She leapt, throwing herself backwards, drawing up her knees. Her buttocks hit the countertop, and the table crashed against the cupboards.

Lacey dropped her feet to the table. Lunging forward, she flung out the contents of the sack. A cloud of flour filled the air.

The man dived through it, an empty shape in the white powder.

Jerking the knife from her mouth, Lacey plunged it into his back. He shrieked. His head drove into her belly, slamming her backwards. Grabbing his shaggy, powdered hair, Lacey tugged away his head. She saw the hazy image of a face, and smashed her fist into its nose. Then she kicked and shoved at the writhing figure until it slid to the floor.

She crawled to the table's edge, and looked down. He was on his knees, head to the floor, growling, reaching behind him with dusty white arms, groping for the knife. His back was half-clear where his blood had swept the flour off.

Lacey jumped, landed beyond him, and fell. Scurrying to her feet, she ran from the kitchen. She grabbed her handbag and keys off the dining room table, and raced into her bedroom. She yanked her bathrobe off the closet hook.

Pulling it on, she ran for the front door. Got outside. Sprinted to her car and locked herself inside and shot it backwards out of the driveway. She hit the brakes. Shifted to Drive. And sped up the road away from her house and the man and the horror.

My God, she thought, I did it!

CHAPTER EIGHT

LACEY ROLLED a clean sheet of paper into her typewriter at the *Tribune* office, and rushed through her story:

Tribune reporter Lacey Allen warded off a masked assailant in her home, Thursday morning, and escaped with minor injuries after stabbing him with a kitchen knife.

According to Miss Allen, the attacker likely concealed himself in the trunk of her car the previous night, after brutally murdering Elsie Hoffman and Red Peterson at Hoffman's Market. 'Some time during the night,' remarks Allen, 'he must have sneaked out of the trunk and broken into my house.'

Awakened in the early morning hours, the young reporter was subdued by the intruder and told that he wished to use her home as a temporary refuge. She was warned of severe consequences if she refused to cooperate.

Later in the morning, while preparing coffee at his request, Miss Allen surprised the suspected killer by flinging flour into his face. Wielding a butcher knife, she attacked and wounded the man, enabling herself to escape.

She sped from the scene in her car. Pulled over by Officer Donald Martin of the Oasis P.D., Miss Allen blurted out her story. The officer radioed for back-up units. Minutes later, officers Martin, Grabowski and Lewis rushed the house, only to find it deserted. A thorough search of the premises and surrounding neighborhood proved fruitless.

Though authorities are baffled by the suspect's disappearance, the incident at Miss Allen's home provides the first clues to his identity. Full sets of fingerprints were discovered at the scene, and have been wired to the F.B.I. headquarters in Washington D.C. for possible identification. Also, impressions of his bare feet were found on the floury kitchen floor, and photographed for later comparisons.

According to Miss Allen, the suspect was a white male in his late twenties, six feet tall, weighing 180 pounds, with long hair. From bits of conversation, Miss Allen feels certain that he is, or has been, a resident of Oasis.

Citizens are urged to exercise extreme caution until the suspect has been apprehended.

Lacey reread her story, then got up from her desk and took the two typewritten pages to Carl Williams. She handed them to the lanky editor, and hiked up her loose corduroys. The rest of the clothes fit no better. Somebody might've at least asked her sizes before sending Alfred out for a new wardrobe. At the time, she'd been too upset to care.

Carl finished reading the story. He rolled back his chair, and frowned. 'Left something out, didn't you?'

'Do *you* believe the guy was invisible?'

'That's what you told me. And the police.'

'But do you believe it?'

He sighed, and rubbed a hand through his short curly hair. 'Hell no,' he said. 'I don't believe it. Not for a second.'

'You figure I imagined it.'

'Well Lace, you've gone through a lot of . . .'

'Slipped a cog or two?'

'I'm not saying that. But it's not unusual for someone – in a car accident, say – to lose her memory of what happened. Goes on all the time.'

'I remember everything.'

'I'm not saying you don't. I'm just saying that, under the circumstances, your sense of reality might've taken a beating.'

'Okay, and that's basically what the cops thought. And it's what our readers will think, too. I have to go on living in this town, Carl. If I claim this guy was invisible, I'll be a joke.'

'Word'll get out, anyway.'

'It'll only be rumor, if it does. I can deny it. But I can't deny something in a story I've written for the *Trib*. Besides, it's not really a lie; I'm pretty sure my description is accurate – as far as it goes. I just can't admit he's invisible, though. I can't. Not in public.'

'Yeah.' He rubbed his face. 'Guess it wouldn't do the *Trib*'s credibility any good, either. Can't have a reporter who *sees* things – or doesn't, as the case may be.' He gave her a weary smile. 'We'll run it this way.'

'Thanks.'

'You'll give me a call when you get to Tucson?'

'Right away.'

'Fine. Take care of yourself, Lace. I'll keep you posted on any new developments.'

'Thanks. See you in two weeks. Sooner, if they get him.'

Lacey went out the rear door to the *Tribune*'s small parking lot. After the air conditioning, the heat outside felt like the breath of an oven. Too bad Alfred didn't buy shorts instead of these corduroys. Squinting against the brilliant glare, she stopped at the rear of her car.

Her stomach fluttered a bit as she opened the trunk. She swept a hand through its emptiness, touched her spare tire, her towel, her flares. Then, satisfied, she shut the trunk and went to the driver's door. She unlocked it, opened it, and reached around to flip up the lock button of the back door.

She opened the door. Crawling over the seat, she reached down and ran her hand along the floor. Then she climbed out, locked and shut the door.

She slid in behind the steering wheel, and locked herself

in. Leaning sideways across the seat, she raked the floor with her fingertips.

Okay.

No passenger.

She started the car, and drove from the parking lot. Her tank was full. She drove for two hours, and didn't stop until she reached the Desert Wind hotel in Tucson.

CHAPTER NINE

'ALFRED, GO on over to Harry's and pick me up some lunch.'

With a nod, Alfred fumbled among half a dozen pens safely clipped inside his plastic pocket shield. He plucked out a Bic, and slipped a note pad from his trousers. 'What'll it be?'

'Pastrami on a sourdough roll, hold the onions. Fries, and a Bud.' Carl waited for the young man to finish scribbling, then gave him a five-dollar bill.

'Want a doughnut or something?'

'Nope.'

'Back in a jiff.'

'No hurry.' Carl followed him outside, watched him start down the sidewalk toward the deli three blocks away, and called after him, 'Don't forget to bring me back some ketchup.'

'Oh, I'll remember.'

He watched Alfred slip the note pad out of his seat pocket. He stepped back inside the office. He shut and locked the door, then hurried through the deserted room to his desk. His hands were sweaty and trembling. He wiped them on his pants legs. He took a deep breath, and picked up the telephone. On the first try, his finger slipped and he had to dial again.

At the other end, the phone rang six times before it was picked up. A woman's pleasant voice said, 'Spiritual Development Foundation, Miss Prince speaking.'

'This is Carl Williams, number 68259385.'

'Just a moment, please.'

He waited for her to punch the code number into her terminal.

'Level?' she asked.

'Red.'

'Very good. What can we do for you, Mr Williams?'

'I have an urgent message for section three.'

'Just a moment, please. I'll put you through to the section three coordinator.'

Carl heard the faint ringing of a phone. Then a strong male voice said, 'Farris, here. What have you got for us?'

'This is Carl Williams, publisher of the *Oasis Tribune*. That's Oasis, Arizona.'

'Right.' He sounded impatient.

'We've had a series of incidents here that I suspect might be related to the SDF – a couple of nasty murders and an assault on one of my reporters, a Miss Lacey Allen.'

'I see. And what makes you think they may be connected to SDF?'

'Oasis is the home town of Samuel Hoffman. Also, Hoffman's mother was one of the murder victims.'

'You think Hoffman may have been the perpetrator?'

'My reporter, Miss Allen, claims that her attacker was invisible.'

'Sounds like our man,' Farris said, sounding pleased. 'Any knowledge of his present whereabouts?'

'Miss Allen wounded him this morning – about four hours ago – at her home here in town. The police couldn't find any trace of him, but I imagine he isn't far from here.'

'Excellent.'

'I may be wrong about this, sir, but I think he's still after the Allen woman. While she was his prisoner, he threatened to hunt her down if she ever escaped.'

'I see. Where is Allen now?'

'She's on her way to Tucson. She took his threat seriously, and plans to hide out there for a while.'

'Her exact location?'

'I don't know. She's promised to give me a call, though,

62

once she's found a room. I suspect she'll check into a hotel.'

'Very good. I'll alert our Tucson personnel. Now. This Allen woman, does she trust you?'

'Yes.'

'As soon as she gives you her location, I want you to do two things. First, inform me immediately. Second, drive to Tucson and meet her. Stay with her, and keep us informed of her movements. If Hoffman goes for her, we want to be there.'

'What if . . . suppose he attacks while I'm there?'

'Any sacrifice you make on our behalf will be rewarded.'

'I mean, do you want me to kill him?'

'Laveda would prefer him alive. It's a moot point, however; you probably couldn't kill him if you tried.'

CHAPTER TEN

A QUIET, rumbling sound entered Dukane's mind. He realized, vaguely, that the sliding glass door to his balcony was being opened. Suddenly alarmed, he tensed and opened his eyes.

It was morning. He stared at the nightstand, thought about jerking open the drawer and grabbing his automatic. Then he remembered bringing a woman home last night from the bar at La Dome. Rolling over, he saw that the other side of the king-size bed was empty.

'Cindy?' he asked.

'Out here.'

He crawled across the bed, climbed off, and saw her standing naked on the sunlit balcony. Her back was toward him, her hands on the railing. He stepped out. The sun felt warm on his bare skin. She looked around and smiled. Kissing her cheek, Dukane pressed himself lightly against her back. He slipped his hands up the smoothness of her sides, and held her breasts.

'It's a lovely day for a swim,' she said.

'If you're planning a dive from here, don't. I tried it once. Broke my ankle.'

'Yuck. I guess I won't.'

'It's farther than it looks, and the concrete is very hard.'

'Were you drunk?'

'When I jumped? Cold sober.'

She sighed as he fingered her rigid nipples. She squirmed, her buttocks rubbing him. Then she turned around. She leaned back against the railings. 'Right here,' she said.

'A bit awkward.'

'Consider it a challenge.'

'I'm always up for a challenge.'

She gripped the railing with both hands and spread her legs. Dukane clutched her hips. Crouching slightly, he found her wet slit. He thrust upward into her. Her head went back and she moaned.

When they were done, they left the balcony. Cindy disappeared into the bathroom. Dukane put on his robe, and went downstairs. He started to prepare coffee. As its thin stream trickled into the pot, Cindy entered the kitchen. She was wearing one of his short-sleeved plaid shirts, and nothing else.

'Okay if I borrow this?' she asked, raising her arms and turning around.

'Wish it looked that good on me.' As he spoke, he remembered Alice wearing one of his spare shirts before he bought the dress for her. He wondered how Dr Teri Miles was faring with her. He didn't envy the woman, spending days alone with the little bitch. Thinking about it, a familiar worry whispered in his mind. He pushed it away. They're all right, he told himself.

'What's your drothers for breakfast?' Cindy asked. 'I make a mean Spanish omelet, if you've got the makings.'

'Hmmm?'

'Spanish omelet. Hello? You tuned in?'

'Yeah. That sounds great. There're chilis in the refrigerator.'

'Cheese, eggs?'

'Them too. You go ahead and get started, I'll bring in the paper.'

'*News*paper?' She wrinkled her nose. 'How dreary.'

'I just read the funnies.'

'Liar liar, pants on fire.'

'Not at the moment.'

With a laugh, she pulled open the refrigerator. She bent over, the tail of the shirt riding up. Dukane glimpsed her pale rump, then turned away.

Outside, he spotted the *Times* halfway up his long driveway. He crossed the lawn, its grass cool and dewy under his feet. The driveway felt pleasantly warm and dry. He picked up the paper. Heading back to the house, he pulled off its plastic ribbon.

The bold letters near the bottom corner of the front page made his heart lurch. 'KABC ANCHORMAN AND WIFE SLAIN.'

He stopped in the wet grass:

KABC news anchorman Ron Donovan and his wife, Ruth, were found brutally murdered last evening in their Hollywood Hills home. The bodies . . .

He didn't read more. He ran to the front door, flung the paper down in the foyer, and raced upstairs. In his bedroom, he grabbed his trousers. He tugged his wallet from the rear pocket, flipped it open, and searched the bill compartment. He pinched out a business card: Dr T R Miles, MD. At the telephone beside his bed, he dialed.

The phone rang fifteen times before he hung up.

In less than a minute, he was dressed. He rushed downstairs.

Cindy was on her knees, reaching into a cupboard, when he entered the kitchen. He patted her bare rump. 'Come on.'

'Huh?'

He held out her panties and skirt. 'Put 'em on, quick. I've gotta get somewhere fast.'

'What's wrong?'

'Just hurry.'

Looking puzzled and worried, she started to get dressed. 'Where're we going?'

'Venice. I have to check on someone.'

She zipped the side of her skirt and followed him to the side door. 'My shoes.'

'You can stay in the car.' He rushed into the connecting garage, climbed into his Jaguar, and pressed the remote button to raise the door. Cindy slid onto the passenger seat as he gunned the engine to life.

'Are you going to tell me what's up?' she asked.

'No,' he said, and sped backwards up the driveway.

'That's a hell of a note.'

'It's business. It's dangerous. You're better off not knowing.' He glanced back to make sure the road was clear, then swung onto it, hit the brakes, and shifted to first gear.

'Then why are you taking me with you?'

'Wouldn't be safe to leave you behind.'

'Safe for who?'

'You.'

'Oh wonderful.'

'It'd probably be all right,' he said, 'but I don't want to take the chance, so it's better if you just stick with me for now.'

'God, what've I got myself into?'

'Consider it an adventure.'

'Maybe you could just drop me off at my apartment, huh?'

'No time.' He sped down the wooded hillside, stopped at Laurel Canyon Boulevard to wait for a break in the traffic, then shot out.

'Look, I'm really not up for an adventure.'

'I'm sorry. Believe me, I was looking forward to your Spanish omelet, a day of swimming and lying in the sun, passionate embraces . . .'

'Me too, damn it.'

'Things go wrong.'

'Yeah. How about letting me out?'

'Barefoot and purseless?'

'Just stop down here at Ventura, and I'll hop out.'

'That's a long hike to Hollywood.'

'I've got a girlfriend. She's only a few blocks away. I'll be fine, thank you.'

Dukane thought it over. He didn't like the idea of dumping her out, but he saw no point in dragging her to Venice, possibly into danger. Steering with one hand, he

67

slipped the wallet from his pocket. He gave it to her. 'Keep that until I get your purse back to you. Collateral.'

'Oh Matt, that's not necessary.'

'There's some cash in it. Use whatever you like.'

She laughed. 'Are you joking?'

'Not at all. Pick up a pair of shoes, treat your friend to lunch, whatever. I'll get your purse and stuff back to you tonight. You'll be home?'

'I'll be there.'

'The address on your driver's license right?'

'Yep.'

The traffic light at the intersection with Ventura Boulevard was red when they reached it. Cindy leaned across the seat, kissed Dukane quickly on the mouth, and sprang from the car.

It took him three freeways and twenty minutes to reach the Lincoln exit in Santa Monica. The traffic on Lincoln was heavy. He finally reached Rose, turned right, and sped up the street for several blocks. He parked on Rose. He ran to the other side, then walked.

Approaching Dr Miles's house, he saw that the gate of its low picket fence stood open. His stomach knotted.

Maybe the mailman had left the gate open.

Wishful thinking.

They got to Alice's parents, found out where she was being kept. No telepathy necessary. No magical powers. Just a check of their records, a visit to the girl's home, an interrogation.

Shit! He'd known, damn it, that something like this could happen. He should've insisted on staying. He'd let the lady talk him out of it, he'd gone against his better judgement, and . . .

The front door stood ajar. Grabbing his automatic, Dukane toed it open. The foyer, the hallway, were deserted. The house was silent.

With his elbow, he eased the door shut. He stepped forward, silent except for the groan of the hardwood floor. At the edge of the living room entry, he stopped. He listened, but heard nothing. Holding his breath, he peered around the corner.

The naked, headless body of a woman was sprawled on the floor, her flesh carved, a fire poker protruding from between her spread legs.

Alice smiled at him. 'I knew you'd come,' she said. She sat cross-legged near the body, her face and yellow sundress smeared with blood. The head of Teri Miles lay in her lap. She lifted it with both hands. The wire rimmed glasses were in place, one lens webbed with cracks. The eyes were open, staring. Alice grinned.

From behind the couch and easy chair, three men rose into view.

'These are my friends. I told you they'd find me.'

'Drop your weapon,' said the man behind the chair. He wore a three-piece suit and a confident smile. In his hand was an automatic, probably .25 caliber, small enough to be concealed easily in a pocket. Too small for much accuracy.

Neither of the others held a gun.

The one on the left, a fat bearded man dressed like a biker, climbed over the back of the couch. He stepped down, his belly swinging, and waved a bloody Bowie knife in front of his smile.

The one on the right stepped around an end of the couch. He wore grease-stained coveralls. He held a pipe wrench.

Dukane took a step into the living room.

'I told you to . . .'

'You drop yours,' he said, raising his .45. 'Mine's bigger.'

The man's eyes flicked to the side. Catching the movement, Dukane whirled around, flung up his left arm, and blocked the knife. The woman wielding it hissed and jerked the blade back, tearing open his forearm. Dukane swung his heavy Colt. It slammed across her cheek and she stumbled backwards, grabbing her face.

Dukane started to turn. He heard a quick flat *bam* like a screen door slamming shut. The bullet punched through his jacket sleeve, but he felt no hit. The clean-cut man tried again as Dukane brought up his automatic and fired. The man's chin dissolved in a burst of red.

Even as the gun bucked, the biker chopped down with his knife. He missed Dukane's wrist, but the powerful blow against the barrel knocked his pistol free. Alice grabbed his ankles. He fell backwards as the huge knife slashed at his belly. Hitting the floor, he jerked a foot free. Alice reached for it. His heel smashed her face aside.

He kicked out at the legs of the biker, but the bulky man lunged forward, kicking back, slashing at his shins.

The grease monkey, at the biker's side, hurled the wrench down at Dukane's head. It almost missed. It numbed his ear and brought tears to his eyes. Dukane grabbed the wrench. He sat up, swinging it to keep away the knife. It clanked against the blade. Before the knife could slash back, he leaned far forward and hammered the man's knee. With a cry of pain, the biker hobbled and fell.

The mechanic was bending down, reaching for Dukane's automatic. Dukane threw the wrench. It bounced off his shoulder, knocking him off balance. As he dropped to one knee, Dukane scrambled toward him. He saw the man pick up the gun, swing its barrel toward him. His fist cut upward. Hit the man's hand. The barrel jumped with the impact, tipped high and blasted a hole through the mechanic's upper teeth. The bullet exited the top of his head, splashing gore at the ceiling.

Dukane jerked the pistol from his dead fingers. He stood as the biker limped toward him, snarling, waving the knife like a pirate's cutlass.

He shot the man in the chest.

The woman who'd caught Dukane's barrel with her cheek was on her hands and knees, spitting blood and bits of broken teeth. She was wearing a tennis dress. Across the seat of her panties was printed 'DON'T POACH'.

Alice lay on the floor, curled up, blood spilling out between the fingers holding her face.

Dukane went to her.

He snapped a handcuff around her left wrist and dragged her across the floor. He cuffed her to the tennis player.

Then he searched for a telephone and called the police.

CHAPTER ELEVEN

LACEY WAS awakened by maids giggling and chattering in the hallway. They spoke Spanish, a language she had picked up as a child in Oasis. She grinned as she listened.

Two of the women had gone on a double-date to the drive-in, last night. Infuriated by their drunken boyfriends, they'd insisted on sitting together. The boyfriends climbed out of the car and went stumbling away, at which point the girls grandly drove off.

Lacey wondered who owned the car.

She flung the sheet aside, and groaned as she sat up. All over her body, her muscles ached with stiffness. She felt better than before, though. Waking up in the hotel room yesterday morning, she'd felt like the loser in a scrimmage with the Dallas Cowboys. Today, by comparison, was great.

Getting off the bed, she hobbled into the bathroom. She studied herself in the full-length mirror. Though her hair was a mess, her face had lost its haggard, haunted look. The bruises mottling her body had turned a sickly, greenish yellow. Hard ridges of scab had formed on her scratches.

'Won't be posing for a centerfold,' she muttered. 'But not bad.'

She took a shower in the huge, glass-sided stall, then dried herself and got dressed in the same baggy clothes Alfred had bought on Thursday.

This was Saturday.

Escape day. Thursday and Friday, she'd been afraid to leave her room. She'd sat around reading paperbacks from the hotel gift shop, watching television, smoking, indulging herself in incredibly expensive food and wine from room service. After two days of it, she was ready to get out. More than ready.

She intended to buy several items, but the sun felt wonderful so she left her car in the hotel parking lot and walked. Three blocks away, in a sporting goods store just off Stone, she found most of what she wanted: a web belt to hold up her corduroys, a tank-top and gym shorts, a one-piece bathing suit, suntan oil, a pocket knife, and a sheath knife with a six-inch blade. After purchasing the items, she shut herself into a dressing room and changed into the shorts and top.

She wandered the downtown area, enjoying the feel of the sun, pleased but slightly nervous with the stares of passing men.

Near noon, she entered a hardware store. She bought a spray can of 'aluminium' colored paint. She ate lunch at a McDonalds, then returned to her hotel.

She put on the swimsuit. With its high neckline, it concealed the worst of her injuries. Scratches and bruises showed on her thighs, her shoulders, her arms. But that couldn't be helped. She was determined to use the pool, no matter how she looked. Turning, she studied her back. The suit left it bare almost to the rump. Her back, at least, looked reasonably unmarred.

She emptied her handbag on the bed, and filled it with what she needed: suntan oil, an Ed McBain paperback, the can of spray paint and her sheath knife. With a bath towel draping her shoulders, she left the room.

The pool, in the hotel's center courtyard, was nearly deserted: a young man was swimming lengths in a steady crawl; a deeply tanned woman lay facedown on a lounge with the top of her black bikini untied; and a middle-aged couple sat beneath an umbrella, sipping Bloody Marys. Lacey spread her towel on a lounge far from the others, and sat down.

She slicked herself with coconut oil, breathing deeply of

its aroma, a rich sweet fragrance that reminded her of other, better times.

Of Will Rogers State Park, near Pacific Palisades where she stayed with Tom and his family that week in spring, six years ago. Her senior year at Stanford. They spent every day at the beach, swimming far out, body surfing, walking the shoreline, or just stretching out on their towels. Tom would trickle coconut oil onto her back. His hands would glide over her, sometimes slipping down between her legs.

Brian used to do that, too, but she never loved Brian. Never loved anyone after Tom. But Brian came along at a time when she needed a man, and she'd never had such sex; Brian cared about nothing else.

Lying back, Lacey sighed and remembered those times by his pool when she lay on her back with her eyes shut and the sun on her naked body – the sun, the oil, and Brian's sliding, searching hands.

Now, she wondered if she could ever allow another man to have her. She knew her desire was strong: it always had been. But could she let herself be touched without recoiling, entered without shuddering in revulsion?

Sprawled on the bathroom floor. The rug against her face. Fingers clamping her shoulders. Erection ramming her.

Hurt by the sudden shock of memory, she opened her eyes, groped inside her handbag, and took out the book. She struggled to read, but her mind soon strayed from the words. She saw herself tied to the bed and she heard the scratchy voice – 'I oughta kill you' – and felt him jerk her legs apart, felt his mouth. She shut the book.

The pool was deserted. The man who'd been swimming lengths now lay on the concrete, dripping, hands folded under his head. Lacey took off her sunglasses. She got up from the lounge and stepped to the pool's edge.

She dived in, jerking rigid at the cold blast of water, gliding through its silence and finally curving upward to the surface. She swam to the far end, turned, and swam back with all her might. Then she turned again and raced to the other end and back. She sidestroked two lengths, then breast-stroked two lengths, then climbed exhausted from the pool. She lowered the back of her lounge and flopped on it facedown, gasping.

She heard the slap of footsteps.

'You're quite a swimmer.'

Raising her head, she looked up at the man – the one who'd been in the pool before her. 'Thanks,' she told him.

'I'm Scott.'

'Hi.'

He was slim and muscular and tanned. His tight bikini trunks covered little of him, and concealed less. He sat on the concrete beside Lacey, facing her. 'Do you have a name?' he asked.

'Doesn't everyone?'

'Oooh. Touchy.'

'Sorry. I'm just not in the mood for company.'

'That's the time when you *need* company the most.'

'Wrong.' She lowered her head, and shut her eyes.

'Can't get rid of me that easily. Nothing I enjoy more than a challenge.'

'Climb a mountain.'

'Too rough. I prefer smoother terrain.'

'Leave me alone, all right?'

'Your back will burn. Would you like me to apply a dab of oil?'

'I wouldn't. I'd like to be left alone. Why don't you go try someone else?'

'Because you're beautiful and lonely.'

Lacey sighed. 'I really don't need this. If you won't leave, I will.'

'Ah, say no more. I can take a hint.'

She opened one eye enough to see him stand. Scott smiled and waved as he backed away.

Resting her head on her crossed arms, Lacey tried to sleep. Her mind replayed the encounter. The guy had been arrogant and pushy. But, damn it, she could've at least been polite. She'd acted like a bitch. She felt herself blushing at the memory.

Well, what's done is done.

She tried not to think about it.

She lay motionless, concentrating on the hot pressure of the sun.

'A libation for the lady.'

Lifting her head, she saw Scott above her, a Bloody Mary in each hand. 'You don't give up, do you?'

'That's why I seldom fail.'

Lacey turned over, stared at the grinning man, and finally sat up. 'I'm Lacey,' she said. 'And I apologize for acting creepy.'

'Creepy is a fair first-line of defense,' he said, sitting down on the concrete. 'Only fair, though. Total complacency works better. It reduces the woman's guilt factor. Much more difficult to penetrate.'

'You've studied the subject.'

'Women fascinate me.' He took the dripping celery stalk from his drink and licked it.

Intentional symbolism? More than likely. Holding back a smile, Lacey removed her own stalk and tapped off its drops on the rim of her glass. She set it down beside her lounge. Scott placed his beside it.

'To our fortunate encounter,' he said.

'Okay.'

He clinked his glass against hers, and they both drank. Her Bloody Mary was hot with tabasco. It made her eyes water, her nose start to run. She sniffed.

'So tell me, Lacey, what is a lovely young lady doing alone at this fashionable resort hotel?'

'What makes you think I'm alone?'

'I have an unerring nose for such things.'

'Unerring?' she asked, somewhat surprised that he had used the correct pronunciation – err as in purr.

'*Seldom* erring. But it's hit the mark this time, hasn't it?'

'Isn't "mark" a conman term for a sucker?'

'Do you see yourself as a sucker?'

'Do you see yourself as a conman?'

He grinned – a boyish, disarming grin. Lacey wondered how much time he spent at mirrors, practicing it. 'A confidence man? Of course. Here I am, trying to win your confidence.'

'When's the pitch?'

'Later. I haven't won yet, have I?'

'Far from it.'

'Are you always this distrustful?'

'Only of strangers who approach me uninvited.'

'Ah. You assume I have mischief on my mind.'

'Do you?'

'That would be telling.'

If I told you that, you'd know. The low, rough voice. She suddenly trembled as if a cloud had smothered the sun, an icy wind blown across her.

'What's wrong?'

'Nothing.'

'Hey, I was only joking about the mischief.'

'I know.'

'Are you all right?'

'I just . . . what you said, it reminded me of something.'

'Must've been something unpleasant.'

'It was.'

'Want to talk about it?'

'No.'

'A chance like this doesn't come along every day, you know: a friendly, willing ear, the sunlight beating down, a Bloody Mary in your hand. Besides, I might be able to help.'

'How could you help?'

'How will I know unless you tell me your problem? Let me guess, though: it involves a man.'

She took a drink, and stared at the glistening pool.

'He did something to you.'

The bantering tone was gone from Scott's voice. Lacey

glanced at him. He was staring at his drink, his face solemn.

'Yes,' she said.

'He didn't jilt you, nothing like that. Whatever he did, you're frightened of him. He hurt you, didn't he? Beat you up.'

'You're very observant,' Lacey muttered, glancing down at her bruises and scratches.

'You came here to get away from him. You're hiding out, probably even registered under a fake name in case he comes looking for you.'

'I couldn't,' she said. 'I had to use a credit card to get the room.'

'But the rest is right?'

'Close enough.' Lacey sipped her drink and set the glass on her belly. Its cold wetness soaked through her damp swimsuit. It felt good.

'Husband, boyfriend, or stranger?'

'Stranger.'

'Did you go to the police?'

'He got away.'

'And you're afraid he'll come after you?'

'He'll kill me, if he can.'

'We won't let him.'

'We?'

He winked. 'You and me, kid.'

'Thanks for the offer, but I don't want anyone else involved in this. Besides, I don't think he'll find me here.'

'It doesn't take a genius to find someone hiding out at a major hotel – particularly if she's using her real name.'

'Thanks.'

'How long have you been here?'

'This is the third day. I got in Thursday afternoon.'

'Then you've been here much too long. You're lucky he hasn't already shown up.'

'He doesn't even know what city I'm in, Scott.'

'You're not from Tucson?'

78

'No.'

'But I'll wager this is the nearest large city, and the place he'll look first.'

'I guess so,' she admitted.

'If I were you, I'd get out of here today and check into a different hotel. Better still, head for another town.'

'It's past check-out time. Besides, I don't want to. I like this one.'

Scott shrugged. 'In that case, I think you should allow me to act as your escort.'

'No. Really, Scott . . .'

'I'd be happy to do it. After all, you're a beautiful woman, and we're both alone in the city. How could I spend my time better than by keeping company with a creature like you?'

'A creature?' she asked, smiling.

'A damsel in distress.'

'It might be dangerous.'

'I'm good with my dukes. Besides, I pack heat.'

'A gun?'

'A Colt .45 automatic. Never go anywhere without it. Except, of course, to the swimming pool.'

'What are you, a bank robber?'

'You ever hear of Charlie Dane?'

'*San Francisco Hit, Manhattan Mayhem . . .?*'

'*Tucson Death Squad.* That's to be his latest battle against the forces of evil. The galleys are up in my suite this very moment.'

Lacey stared at him, frowning. 'But those are written by Max Carter.'

'Otherwise known as Scott Bradley.'

'You.'

'Me.'

'That still doesn't explain the gun.'

'Max keeps the rod at his side when he sits at the old typewriter. It puts him in touch with Charlie Dane.'

Lacey grinned. 'Does Max also wear Charlie's trench coat?'

'Too hot. But he does don the battered fedora.'
'Not while he's escorting me, I hope.'
'I'll leave Max in the room, and borrow his piece.'
'He won't mind?'
'He's always eager to please.'

CHAPTER TWELVE

CARL GRABBED the phone before its second ring. '*Tribune.*'

'Carl?'

His heart began to hammer. 'How's it going, Lace?'

'So far, so good. He hasn't found me yet. Any activity on your end?'

'Nope. There haven't been any incidents since you left.'

'Damn. I almost wish . . . At least I'd know he's still there.'

'Well, maybe he's just lying low. Or maybe your knife did the trick.'

'Don't I wish.'

'So, how are you feeling?'

'Scared. Other than that, I guess I'm all right. Recuperating.'

'That's good. Look, you'd better let me know where you're staying. If something breaks, up this way, I'll want to let you know.'

'Sure. I'm at the Desert Wind, room three sixty-two.'

Carl wrote it down.

'I meant to call you yesterday, but . . . couldn't get myself to do anything. Felt like crawling under a rock.'

'That's all right, Lace. Perfectly understandable.'

'Anyway, I'm better now.'

'Glad to hear it. Look, is there anything I can do for you?'

'Just keep me posted, is all.'

'Sure thing. Take care of yourself, now.'

'I'll try. So long, Carl.'

He hung up. Across the room, one of his reporters hunched over a typewriter working on the lead story for tomorrow's edition. Otherwise, the office was deserted. 'Jack?'

The reporter looked up, raising his eyebrows.

'See if you can't hunt down Chief Barrett. Try to talk him into letting us release the details of the Hoffman and Peterson murders.'

'He's already refused, Carl.'

'Try him again. Tell him a blow by blow description would be in the public interest, make them more aware of the danger. Maybe he'll go for it.'

'Okay,' Jack said, sounding reluctant. He pushed his chair back, stood up, and stretched. Then he headed for the door.

The moment he was gone, Carl dialed the telephone.

'Spiritual Development Foundation.'

He gave his name, number and level.

'Very good, Mr Williams.'

'Let me talk to Farris. It's urgent.'

Farris's voice came over the phone. 'We've been waiting for your call,' he said.

'Sorry. I just received the information. Miss Allen's at the Desert Wind Hotel in Tucson. Room number three six two.'

'Excellent. I'll notify our personnel in the area. Your next step is to join her.'

'Right.'

'Do that at once.'

'I'll leave right away.'

As he hung up, a voice from behind asked, 'What was that all about?'

Carl swiveled around. Alfred, standing in front of the restroom door, looked at him with suspicion. 'You told where Lacey is. Who'd you tell?'

'Chief Barrett.'

'What'd you want to do that for?'

'She asked me to.' Turning back to his desk, Carl pulled open the top drawer and removed a letter opener. 'Bring me Jack's story,' he said.

Alfred walked toward Jack's desk, his head low and shaking. 'I don't think you should've done that,' he said.

'You're not paid to think.'

'Well . . .' He gathered two pages from the desktop, and walked slowly back toward Carl.

Carl got up from his chair. With the letter opener behind his back, he reached out his left hand for the papers.

'Here they . . .'

Carl grabbed Alfred's wrist, jerked him forward, and plunged the slim blade into his belly.

CHAPTER THIRTEEN

A STROLLING guitarist stopped at their table. 'A song?'

Scott nodded. 'How about "Cielito Lindo"?' he asked Lacey.

She dipped a tortilla chip into hot sauce. 'Fine.'

With a smile, the white-clothed Mexican began to strum chords and sing. Lacey sat back, munching her chip and sipping her margarita as she watched him. He stood with his back arched, his head thrown back, his dark face writhing as if the song called up unbearable sorrow. His plaintive voice pushed Lacey's mind back to a strolling minstrel in Nogales, only a few days before her break-up with Brian. One of their last good times together. The next week, back in Oasis, he brought a man to the house and insisted the three of them go at each other. Lacey refused, and he beat her. No more Brian. No more men, at all, after that.

For a moment, she felt the void and sank into it. No man, no love, no babies, only empty darkness. She was cut loose and drifting. Starting to panic.

She took a long drink from her margarita, and managed a smile for Scott.

Get off it, kiddo, she told herself. A hell of a time to worry about becoming an old maid. You should live so long.

The singer finished his song, and Scott handed him a dollar.

'*Gracias*,' the man said. With a slight bow, he turned away.

'Are you all right?' Scott asked.

'Just beweeping my outcast state.'

Scott raised an eyebrow. 'Troubling deaf heaven with your bootless cries?'

Lacey grinned. 'Yup.'

The waitress set down plates in front of them. They had both ordered Dinner #6: a chimichanga, refried beans, rice, and a taco. Lacey took a deep breath of the steam rising from her meal. Her mouth watered.

'Plates are hot,' warned the waitress. 'Will there be anything else for you?'

'Want a beer?' Scott asked.

'I'll stick with margaritas.'

'That'll be it for now,' he told the waitress, and she left.

Across the candle-lit room, the singer began 'The Rose of San Antone' for two lean men in business suits. One of them saw Lacey watching. He met her gaze, looked her over, then turned away and spoke to his friend. The other man glanced at her. She looked away, embarrassed, certain they were wondering about her appearance. In her plaid blouse and corduroys, she felt shabby: all right for McDonalds, but barely good enough for a restaurant of Carmen's quality.

She should've found time to buy a dress. When Scott escorted her back to her suite that afternoon, though, he gave her strict orders not to leave it without calling him. She hadn't wanted to drag him around Tucson in search of evening wear, so she'd simply stayed in her room until he picked her up for dinner. Now, she regretted it.

She swallowed a mouthful of rice, and said, 'What's next?'

'Find a good piano bar . . .'

'I mean, tomorrow and the next day and the day after that.'

'Depends on you.'

'Are we just going to *wait*? I mean, I could stay at the hotel for two weeks, as I planned, and nothing happen, and the minute I step into my house back in Oasis, *wham*.'

'You think he's at your house?'

'He could be anywhere: in my house, at the hotel, even

here. He might even be dead, but I think that's too good to hope for.'

'So you don't want to wait around? You'd rather go on the offensive? Good. That's just what Charlie Dane would suggest.'

'Are you willing?' she asked.

'I was planning to suggest it, myself.'

She cut into the chimichanga with her fork, and scooped a bite into her mouth. The fried tortilla crunched. She chewed slowly, savoring its spicy meat and cheese.

'So tomorrow, we'll go to your house.'

'That'd be great.' Lacey took another bite. Then she picked up her handbag and set it on her lap. She opened it. She took out the can.

'What's that, paint?'

'There's something you have to know. You may decide I'm crazy and call the whole thing off, but I have to tell you the truth. This afternoon, when I explained the whole situation to you, I left something out. It's why I have this paint. I told you the man was wearing a mask. That's my story for public consumption, but it's not quite the truth. I told the truth to the police and my editor, and they didn't believe me. I don't really expect you to believe me, either. But here goes. The man who killed Elsie Hoffman and Red Peterson, the man who attacked me – he's invisible.'

Scott stared at his plate. He forked a huge bite of chimichanga into his mouth, and chewed slowly, frowning. He swallowed. He finished his margarita and refilled the glass and took another sip. 'Invisible?' he asked, as if he thought he'd misunderstood.

'Not a ghost or apparition or hallucination,' Lacey said. 'It's a man. But you can look right at him and see right through him and never know he's even there. He's invisible.'

'How?' Scott asked.

'He didn't tell me. "A little miracle," he said.'

'A miracle, all right.'

'That's what the paint is for. It'll adhere to him, and he

won't be invisible again till he gets it off his skin.'

'Invisible,' Scott said, shaking his head.

'Do you believe me?'

'Let me put it this way: we'll proceed as if I do. Hell, if it's true, I might get a whizz-bang story out of this. Another *Amityville Horror*. Who knows?'

Back at the hotel, Scott drew a Colt .45 automatic from the shoulder holster under his sports coat.

They searched Lacey's suite, walking behind chairs, feeling inside closets and under the beds, stepping into the shower stall. At last, Scott sighed and sat on the couch. 'If the guy's invisible,' he said, 'there's no way we can be sure he isn't here.'

'He hasn't attacked,' Lacey said.

'Maybe he's waiting for me to leave. So I guess I'd better stay.' He patted the couch. 'This'll do fine.'

'You're really going to stay?'

'I can't do much protecting from the end of the hall.'

'Well, I guess it's all right. I won't let you sleep on the couch, though, with two beds in the other room.'

'You sure?'

'It'd be ridiculous.'

Grinning, Scott drawled, 'Mighty grateful, ma'am. I accept your hospitality.'

Lacey went to bed first. Though she usually slept in the nude, tonight she wore her jogging shorts and tank top in case her sheet should slip off during the night. She lay wide awake. From the other room came quiet T.V. voices. She listened, but couldn't make out their words.

Had it been a mistake, offering the other bed? It might've sounded like an invitation for something more. Had Scott taken it that way? God, what if he came over to her bed and climbed in?

He would say something cute. 'I'm here to guard your body at close range.'

She rolled onto her belly, and forced her mind away from the possibility. How'll we work it in the morning?

Each drive our own cars, I suppose. Meet at my house. We'll park in front. Go in together? Sneak in? And search the place. Spread flour around so we can see footprints? God, what a clean-up job. Would it come out of the carpet?

The television voices stopped.

Lacey heard quiet footsteps. She expected Scott to enter the bathroom just off the hallway, but the steps kept coming. The doorknob rattled a bit. Then the door swung open.

She pressed her face against the pillow and shut her eyes.

Please, let him go straight to his own bed.

I'm here to guard your body at close range.

The footsteps stopped between the beds. She heard the squeak of springs, followed by a whispered 'damn' as if he were angry about the noise. Obviously, he thought she was asleep and didn't want to disturb her. So he had no intention of coming to her bed, after all.

Lacey remained motionless, listening to his breathing, to the quiet sounds the bed made as he shifted to remove his shoes, to the single tink of his belt buckle and the whisper of his zipper. Then the springs squawked.

He's standing up.

Coming here, after all? Lacey's heart began to thunder.

Turning her head slightly, she opened one eye and saw him in the darkness only a yard away. He stepped out of his pants, folded them once, and placed them on the floor beside his bed. He took off his shoulder holster, then his shirt. His tanned skin looked very dark against his white briefs. Crouching, he folded his shirt and set it on top of the pants. Then he turned away to pull down the bed covers. He climbed in without taking off his shorts.

Lacey shut her eye. Her heart was still racing, and she realized that she'd barely been breathing since Scott entered the room.

She was parched. She tried to work up enough saliva to moisten her mouth, but couldn't.

She waited.

I'll die if I don't get a drink of water. Probably those margaritas.

Slipping her sheet aside, she swung her legs off the bed and stood up. She rushed through the darkness to the bathroom, and turned on a light. Squinting against its glare, she ran cold water. She filled a glass and drank. In the mirror, she saw hair clinging to her sweaty forehead. She shook her head at the image. She drank another glassful of cold water, then turned off the faucet and used the toilet. The flush sounded very loud. If Scott heard it . . . No, he's all right. He'll stay in bed. If he'd wanted to try anything tonight, he would've done it by now.

She flicked off the light and opened the door.

Scott clutched her shoulders. He was wearing only his briefs. In his right hand, upraised to his shoulder, he held the pistol. It smelled oily and metallic.

'What . . .?'

'Shhhh. We've got company.'

CHAPTER FOURTEEN

STANDING CLOSE to Scott in the dark hallway, Lacey heard the quiet rap of knuckles on wood. 'Where's it coming from?' she asked.

'Our door.'

'You sure?'

Scott nodded.

'My God.'

'Come on.' Holding her by the elbow, Scott led her into the main room. They stood motionless. After a moment of silence, the knocking resumed. 'I'll watch from the closet,' Scott whispered. 'You get the door.'

'What if it's *him*?'

'Then we're in luck.'

As Scott hurried to the coat closet, Lacey turned on a lamp. 'Right there,' she called. She scanned the room, and found her handbag on the coffee table. Rushing to it, she took out the can of spray paint and the knife. She pulled off the leather sheath, and slid the knife under the waist band at the back of her shorts. The blade was cool and flat against her rump. She felt the scrape of its edges as she walked to the door.

She peered through the peephole. Though the man in the bright hallway looked shrunken and distorted as if viewed in a distant funhouse mirror, Lacey recognized his lanky build, his haggard face and short, curly hair.

'Carl?'

She flicked off the guard chain, and pulled the door open. Carl gazed at her with grim, red-rimmed eyes. 'Hi, Lace.'

90

'Carl, what's going on? What're you doing here?'

'I'm sorry. Did I wake you?'

'No. Come on in.'

Lacey stepped aside to let him enter. Then she shut and chained the door. She turned to him. 'Did something happen? What's wrong?'

'Our man paid a visit to the *Trib*. He . . . he killed Alfred.'

'Oh my God!'

'I came back from lunch, and . . . Alfred was on the floor.' Reaching into a pocket of his baggy slacks, Carl pulled out a folded sheet of paper. 'The police have the original. It was pinned to him, to his belly . . . with my letter opener.' He handed the paper to Lacey.

She set the spray can on the coffee table, and unfolded the paper, and stared. The photocopy was stained as if it had been used to mop up a spill of black ink. But the typing was legible. She read it in silence. 'Can't get rid of me that easy. Better come home, bitch, or your editor's next.' With a trembling hand, she gave the note back to Carl.

'I thought I'd call you, but . . . Hell, I remembered what you said about him being invisible. Still not sure I can believe that, but I figured I'd better be careful. If he *is* like you say, he might've been right behind me, watching me dial. If he got the hotel's number . . . Well, I figured I'd drive on out to be on the safe side.'

'He could've been in your car!' Lacey blurted, suddenly alarmed.

'No. I checked it over.'

'Your trunk?'

'Checked that, too.'

'Maybe he followed you.'

'I don't think so. Wasn't much traffic. The only car behind me much had a couple in it – a man driving, a woman passenger.' He made a grim smile. 'Neither one was invisible. So I think we're okay on that score.'

'You saw the man's face?' Lacey asked.

'Not up close, but he had one. It's all right, Lace. Now stop worrying. I wasn't followed.'

'He could've put something on. A mask, make-up . . .'

Carl shook his head. 'We've gotta figure out what to do about this guy. Seems to me, we're both in the same boat, now. I don't think I want to hang around Oasis and just wait for him to slit my gullet. I figure, if we stick together on this . . .'

'What about the woman passenger?' Lacey asked.

'Huh?'

'In the car that followed you.'

'It wasn't *following* me. It was just *behind* me.'

'All the way?'

'I don't know.' He sounded annoyed. 'I didn't keep track. It was just some clown and his wife.'

'How do you know it was his wife?'

' 'Cause,' Carl said, smiling slightly, 'she was asleep the whole way.'

'*Asleep?*'

'Sure. Slumped over, her head against the side window . . . Oh, for Christsake, Lace, don't turn paranoid on me. Don't start telling me she was dead, and the driver was your invisible man decked out in a Stetson and mask.'

'You think that's not possible?'

'I think you're jumping to some mighty big conclusions.'

'He figured you would know where to get in touch with me. Killing Alfred, leaving the note, he did it so you'd lead him here. For Godsake, he's probably . . .'

'Now don't get all worked up. Calm down. There's nothing to . . .'

Lacey jerked stiff as her knife turned, the blade slicing a white-hot line up her buttock. She clutched the wound and spun around. The suspended knife slashed through the air, barely missing her face, and jerked toward Carl.

'*Scott!*'

The closet door burst open. Scott crouched, pistol forward, but his face was twisted with confusion. '*Where?*'

Even as Lacey pointed, the blade punched into Carl's

throat. Blood shot out. It spurted a few inches, then splattered as if hitting a sheet of glass. It sprayed and sheathed the surface – the face and shoulders and chest of a six-foot man.

Scott gazed, his mouth agape.

'Shoot him!'

The figure, vague as a patch of floating red cellophane, raised Carl off his feet and flung him at Scott. Scott leapt sideways. The body hit the closet door, crashed it shut, and thudded to the floor. The knife, Lacey saw, was still embedded in Carl's throat.

Scott aimed at the film of blood rushing toward him. 'Stop!'

Lacey braced herself for the roar of gunfire. It didn't come.

A yard in front of Scott, the figure halted.

'Fuckin' blood,' muttered a scratchy voice.

The layer of red shifted as if a child were fingerpainting on his face.

'Hands on your head,' Scott ordered.

The top of the head wasn't there, but Lacey saw two hand-shaped images of blood suspended above the concave face – a face like the back of a translucent red Halloween mask.

Lacey grabbed her can of silver paint from the coffee table and tugged off its plastic top. Tossing the cap aside, she shook the can. It rattled as if a marble were trapped inside. She stepped close to the dripping, red veil in front of Scott's automatic.

'Don't do it,' the man muttered.

As her forefinger lowered to the plastic nozzle, the red membrane shifted like a flag struck by wind. Something struck Lacey's hand. The can tumbled away. Then a tightness clenched her wrist and swung her toward Scott. He jumped out of the way, rushed in front of her, and dived. He landed flat on the floor, his hands grabbing only air.

The door flew open, ripping the guard chain from its mounting, and slammed shut.

Scott pushed himself to his knees. His eyes met Lacey's. He shook his head.

Lacey stepped over to Carl's body. She knelt down beside him. Blood no longer pumped from his torn throat. She covered her face with both hands, and started to cry.

CHAPTER FIFTEEN

LACEY LAY face down on the livingroom floor, her shorts around her knees, Scott patting her cut buttock with a cool, damp washcloth. 'Not much bleeding,' he said. 'You don't have bandages or anything, do you?'

'Afraid not.'

'Have any sanitary napkins?'

She felt heat flood her face, and wondered if the blush extended to her rump. 'Not with me.'

'Well, it's not much more than a scratch, but . . .'

'Oh, I think there *is* a pad in the medicine cabinet. The hotel variety. Right behind some kind of shower cap and shoeshine rag.'

'Advantages of a first-rate hotel,' Scott said, and left her. He returned, seconds later, tearing open the white wrapper. He knelt down, and pressed the soft pad against her wound. 'The tape's on the wrong side,' he muttered.

'Supposed to be. My underwear'll hold it in place.'

'Oh.' He went for her panties, and hurried back.

'Thanks,' Lacey said. 'I can take care of the rest.'

While she pulled on her panties and shorts, Scott went into the hallway. He came back with a blanket.

He used it to cover the body of Carl Williams. Dots of blood darkened the fuzzy pink blanket, bloomed, and grew together. Lacey turned away.

She got to her feet. Wandering to a far corner of the room, she picked up the can of spray paint. She sat gently on the couch, clutching the can with both hands.

Scott sat beside her. 'I screwed up,' he said. 'I'm sorry. I thought everything was okay until you yelled. Then I couldn't find a target.' Shaking his head, he sighed. 'Christ, what a screw up. I'm sorry about your friend. If I'd just been . . .'

'Don't blame yourself. Nobody could've stopped it, at that point.'

'Charlie Dane could've,' he mumbled.

'Charlie would've shot the bastard when he had the chance,' Lacey said.

'Yeah.'

'The bastard's out there, now. He's had time to get the blood off.'

'Yeah.'

'Why didn't *you* shoot him?'

For a long time, Scott stared at the coffee table.

'Scott?'

'I thought we had him. I figured we'd tie him up. I've got a cassette recorder in my room. I thought . . . well, I'd get his story. You know, before calling in the cops. Interview him, find out how he got that way, what he's been doing, if there are others like him.'

'Others?'

'If one man can be made invisible, why not more? Christ, can you imagine an army of them? Think what they could do. They could turn the world upside down.'

'I suppose so,' Lacey said. 'But there's only one here, and he's probably figuring a way, right now, to get at us. You aren't going to have much luck writing a book about him if we're both killed, so next time . . . My God!' Jumping to her feet, she rushed to the desk and grabbed a straight-backed chair.

'What?'

She ran to the door with it, tipped it backwards and braced it under the knob. 'Maybe that . . .' she muttered. She turned to Scott. 'A passkey. He could get one so easily.'

Scott sighed. 'Damn, I should've thought of that. Afraid I'm not helping much.' He looked at her with despair. 'Sorry. I'm really not good enough for this kind of thing.

Living it isn't quite the same as writing it.' He propped his elbows on his knees, and rubbed his face.

Lacey went to him. Crouching, she placed a hand on his back. 'Hey, it's all right. Don't feel bad. If you hadn't been here, he would've had me.'

Scott raised his head and looked at her. 'Thanks.'

'It's the truth. You saved my life.'

He smiled slightly. 'You're right.'

'Of course I am.'

'But I'm right, too,' he said. His face changed, turning hard and determined. 'This is out of my league. I'm not going to let my inexperience jeopardize you any longer.' He touched her cheek, stood up, and walked toward the desk.

'What are you doing?'

'Calling in reinforcements,' he said, and picked up the telephone. He set his automatic on the desk, then dialed with quick, sure strokes of his forefinger. Eleven numbers.

Long distance?

CHAPTER SIXTEEN

THE BEDSIDE telephone woke Dukane, and he saw a naked woman bending over him in the darkness. Her head jerked toward the phone. In the moments between the clamors of the first and second rings, Dukane realized that the woman – a stranger before he brought her home tonight – had been interrupted in the process of tying his left wrist to the headboard.

He yanked both arms. The headboard shook and a cord bit into his right wrist, but his left pulled free.

The woman grabbed it, tried to force it down.

'Thanks,' Dukane said, 'but I'm not into bondage.'

He twisted his arm out of her grip. As the woman reached for it again, he clutched her neck and thrust her forward, ramming her head against the oak of his headboard. She slumped. He shoved her off the bed, rolled to his right, and picked up the phone.

'Hello?'

'Dukane? It's Scott. I'm in deep trouble, pal.'

'What's the problem?'

'There's a killer after me. An invisible killer.'

'Invisible?'

'I know it sounds ridiculous, but believe me, it's true. He just murdered a guy here in the room.'

'Okay. Where are you?'

'The Desert Wind hotel in Tucson. Room three sixty-two.'

'Where's this killer?'

'Probably right outside the door.'

'Okay. Hang tough, kid, I'm on my way. It'll take me

about four hours, though. Maybe less, but don't count on it.'

'Hurry.'

'Right.' Dukane hung up. He slid open a drawer of the night stand, took out a switchblade knife, and severed the cord binding his right hand to the headboard. Then he turned on a light. He climbed across the bed and knelt over the unconscious woman.

She lay on her back, breathing deeply as if asleep, her arms and legs outflung. A beautiful, slim, small-breasted blonde. Just his type. Too much his type, perhaps. But he'd known a lot of women over the years, and only a handful had turned out to be plants. He should've been a lot more careful, after Friday's disaster. He should've expected something like this.

Confidence kills.

She began to stir, her eyelids squeezing tight with a stab of pain, a hand rising to her head. She pursed her lips and said, 'Oooh.' Then her eyelids fluttered open. She gazed at Dukane with confusion for a moment before her memory apparently returned and she bolted upright.

Dukane clutched her throat and slammed her down. 'Who sent you?'

She sneered. 'No one.'

'I don't have time for games.' He jabbed his knife down. Her body jerked as if jolted by a cattle prod, mouth springing open to scream. He stopped the point of his knife above her bulging right eye. An eighth of an inch above it. She blinked, her lashes flicking over the steel tip. 'Who sent you?'

She said nothing. Slowly, the panic left her face. Her body relaxed. Even the straining tendons and muscles of her neck went slack under Dukane's hand. She smirked up at him. 'Do as you like,' she said. 'Cut out my eye, if that's what pleases you. Take whatever you wish. My breasts?' Her hands moved, stroking them. The dark nipples stood rigid. 'I am all powerful,' she whispered. 'I am immortal.'

'Have you drunk at the river?' Dukane asked.

'Oh yes, oh yes.'

He eased the blade away from her eye.

'Immortal,' she said. 'All powerful.'

He removed his right hand from her throat. 'Okay, get up.' As he inched the knife away, her fingers caught his wrist. Dukane tensed, expecting an upward thrust. But she tugged down. He wasn't ready for that. The blade punched into the pale flesh between her breasts.

Dukane snatched it free.

The woman bucked, clutched the wound, and sat up with a look of sudden terror on her face.

Blood spilled out between her fingers. She glanced at it, then gazed at Dukane with eyes like a hurt child.

'Shit,' Dukane muttered, suddenly feeling sorry for her. 'Don't worry, you missed your heart. I'll call an ambulance.' He rushed around the end of the bed. 'Press down hard on the wound.' He picked up the phone.

As he started to dial, the woman grabbed the bed and pushed herself to her feet.

'Lie down, damn it!'

She suddenly ran.

'Hey!' Dukane dropped the phone and scrambled over the bed, hoping to stop her before she reached the sliding door to the balcony.

She was too quick.

Her forehead rammed the door. The plate glass burst. She lunged through a spray of tumbling shards that slashed her bare skin, and disappeared onto the balcony. Dukane rushed after her. As he ducked through the smashed door, she threw herself headfirst over the railing. Dukane lunged, reached for her foot, and touched its heel with his forefinger. Then all he could do was watch.

She kicked and twisted for a second that seemed like minutes even to Dukane, then threw out her arms to break her fall. The concrete slab of the pool's apron smashed her arms out of the way, and she hit it with her face.

Dukane looked down at her body, and sighed. He knew

he shouldn't feel sorry for her; she'd probably planned to kill him tonight. But Christ, the waste . . . a beautiful girl . . . Why the hell did she ever get mixed up in such . . .

He clutched the railing, frozen by a sudden chill as a huge, black-robed man darted from behind bushes beside the pool. The man crouched at the broken body, flung it over his shoulder, and lumbered away.

Dukane pried his fingers off the railing. His skin was crawly with goosebumps. He stared down at the dark figure and knew he should give chase, but he couldn't move.

Besides, he told himself, Scott has priority. He watched, rubbing his prickly arms and thighs, thinking it strange that he should be so spooked. Whoever the bastard was, Dukane could probably nail him in unarmed combat, even with one hand tied behind his back. Probably. The thought didn't give him much comfort.

He picked bits of glass out of his feet, then hobbled down the long balcony to its guest room entrance. He slid open the door and stared at the pale carpet.

'Shit,' he muttered.

One ruined carpet was enough for one night.

On hands and knees, keeping his feet elevated, he crawled across the carpet. In the guest bathroom, he found iodine, adhesive tape, and gauze. He quickly bandaged his feet.

Ignoring the slight pain, he rushed back to his bedroom. He glanced at the clock. Less than five minutes had passed since Scott's call.

A long time, five minutes.

A long time for that dumb woman. A long time for a guy like Scott, waiting to get bailed out.

It took him under a minute to dress.

Then he ran downstairs, through the dark house, and out to his garage. He jumped into his Jaguar. Thumbed the garage door switch. Keyed the ignition. The engine thundered, shaking the car.

In his rearview mirror, he watched the door rise. The

gap widened. He saw the dark-robed man looking in at him, the naked body of the girl still over his shoulder.

Dukane jammed the shift to reverse and floored the gas pedal. He popped the clutch. The car leapt backwards. He gripped the wheel, expecting an impact, but the car shot past the figure. Caught in the headlight, the man turned slowly to face him.

Dukane's foot hovered over the brake. He could easily stop and have another try.

But Scott was waiting.

He'd already wasted too many minutes.

So he sped backwards to the street, leaving the strange man alone in the driveway with the corpse.

CHAPTER SEVENTEEN

'WHAT WAS that about?' Lacey had asked as soon as Scott put down the phone.

'Saving our hides.'

'Dukane? Who's he?'

'The real-life Charlie Dane. Excuse me a minute, I want to get dressed.' He left her alone in the room.

Lacey got up and followed him. When she reached the bedroom, Scott was stepping into his pants. 'There really *is* a Charlie Dane?'

Scott fastened his trousers and picked up his shirt. 'Sure is. No trench coat and battered fedora, and he operates now instead of the forties, but the rest is pretty close. A hell of a guy. He'll get us out of here. We just have to stay alive for the next four hours, till he arrives.'

'Maybe we should call the police.'

'What good would they be against an invisible maniac?'

'What good will this Dukane be?'

Scott grinned, for the first time since the attack looking calm and confident. 'Good enough.'

'What time is it?' Lacey asked.

'Eleven-forty.'

'Is that all?' Only twenty minutes had passed since Scott's talk with Dukane. For the past ten, Lacey had been sitting cross-legged beside the barricaded door, her pocket knife open on her lap, the paint can beside her ready to spray if the door should be forced open.

Scott had spent much of the time wandering the suite. He'd looked out the windows and determined that no ledges ran over from adjacent rooms. He'd shoved the couch against a locked, connecting door. Then he'd knelt down to remove the knife from Carl's throat.

'Should you do that?' Lacey had asked. 'What about fingerprints?'

'We need it.'

'But the police. My God, we don't want them thinking *we* killed Carl.'

'Don't worry.'

'Thanks, but I can't help it.'

'The police are the least of our problems, right now.'

Lacey had looked away when he pulled out the knife. He arranged the blanket again over Carl's head, then took the knife into the bathroom and cleaned it.

Now Scott was turning over the coffee table.

'What're you doing?'

'Clubs,' he said, and began to unscrew one of the short, tapering legs. When it came free, he tossed it underhand. It thumped the floor near Lacey, and rolled toward her. She picked it up by the narrow end. It felt like a small baseball bat. A thick, inch-long bolt protruded from the top.

As Scott twisted another leg off the table, Lacey heard voices in the hallway.

'Six fifty for a Piña Colada,' said a man. 'You believe it?'

'That's not so bad,' a woman said. 'It included the glass.'

'Sixty cents worth of glass. A nickle worth of booze.'

'They're awfully cute glasses.'

'Maybe we should get a few more.'

'It would be nice to have a complete set.' The woman's sudden yelp made Lacey jump. Her mind flashed an image of the two under attack, and she grabbed the spray can, tensing, ready to unblock the door and rush out to help. But the yelp led into a giggle. A different kind of attack. 'Jimmy, *don't!* Christ, I almost dropped the glasses.'

'Anything but that.'

Lacey heard a key ratchet into a lock. A knob turned.

A door swung open with a barely audible squeak, and banged shut.

'Hope they got in alone,' Scott said, starting on a third leg.

'I sure hope so. They sounded nice.'

'The guy's a cheapskate.'

'He was just kidding around.'

'Yeah. On the surface. Underneath, he's a cheapskate.'

'He did buy two of those drinks.'

'At six-fifty a whack. Not only a cheapskate, but he likes to play martyr.'

Lacey looked at Scott, and saw he was smiling.

The door's lock button snapped out. Lacey turned, saw the door lurch, the chair tip forward a fraction. She thrust herself to her knees. The knife fell from her lap. She grabbed it. Scott threw himself against the wall on the other side of the door. He held a table leg in one upraised hand, the knife in the other. The automatic remained tucked in his belt.

The door eased back silently, then rammed the chair again, this time forcing the legs to scoot an inch across the carpet.

'Shoot him through the door,' Lacey whispered.

Scott shook his head. 'Louder,' he mouthed.

'Shoot through the door!'

'Right.' Clamping the club between his legs, he pulled out the automatic. He held it close to the door and worked its slide, jacking a live cartridge out.

The door settled back into place.

Lacey waited, holding her breath, expecting another thrust. Scott picked up his bullet and dropped it into his shirt pocket.

Nothing happened.

'Whatever he is,' Scott whispered, 'he doesn't like bullets.' Tucking away the pistol, he shoved the chair more firmly under the knob. 'I think we're all right for a while . . . till he figures a new way to get at us.'

'What'll he do?'

Scott shrugged.

'What time is it now?'

Scott glanced at his wristwatch. 'Five minutes later than the last time you asked.'

'Encouraging,' she muttered.

'Three and a half hours to go.'

'If your man's on time.'

'Knowing Dukane, he'll be early.'

'I hope so.' Lacey sat down again, feeling a slight pain as her shorts drew taut across her wound. Raising herself for a moment, she tugged the shorts to loosen them. Fortunately, the cut was high enough so that she didn't rest on it, sitting upright. It hurt very little, except for a frequent, achy itch. It itched now. She scratched it gently with her fingernails. 'What makes you think this Dukane will do us any good?'

'He's brilliant, innovative, a crack shot . . .'

'Able to leap tall buildings in a single bound?'

'Damn near. Won the Medal of Honor in Vietnam. Dropped in behind the lines, killed God-knows how many gooks, freed two dozen POWs and led them all back. Alone.'

Scott shook his head, looking astonished by the feat. 'He's been a private investigator and bodyguard for nine years. An amazing guy. He's actually lived the Charlie Dane stories. Most of them are based on incidents from Dukane's past.'

'Hope I live long enough to meet him.'

'I keep trying to figure out what he'd do, if he were here instead of me.'

'What would he do?'

Scott shook his head. One corner of his mouth smiled. 'He'd make clubs out of the table legs.'

'Would he shoot through the door?'

'More than likely.'

'I wish you had.'

'Don't tell anyone, but my shooting has been limited to pistol ranges. I've never killed a man.'

'That would've been a good time to start.'

'Well . . .' Scott sighed. 'I'm not against it – morally, I mean. Sort of a big step, though. Besides, I'd still rather take him alive. I mean, can you imagine the *story*? It'd be terrific! Do it up non-fiction. A hardbound sale. Major advertising and promotion. Whammo, a bestseller!'

'Give *me* your gun,' Lacey said, scrambling to her feet. She held out her hand. 'Come on, give it. If you aren't willing to shoot him, I sure am.'

He held onto it. 'Sorry.'

'Sorry won't get us out of a coffin. Now come on! You've missed two big chances to blast this bastard to hell. Let *me* do it.'

'Lacey, don't get . . .'

She lunged, reaching for the automatic. Scott knocked her arm away. He shoved her backwards with the table leg, its bolt biting into her chest. 'Calm down!'

'You'll get us killed!' she blurted, and suddenly started to cry. She turned away. She wanted to run for the bedroom or bathroom, to let out her despair in private, but was afraid to leave him. So she faced the wall, crying into her hands. She heard Scott approach. His arms reached forward and folded lightly across her belly.

'I won't let anything happen to you,' he said, his breath warm through her hair. 'I promise.'

'What about your bestseller?'

'I won't let him get you.'

Lacey turned around. Blinking tears away, she stared up into his serious eyes. 'You could shoot to wound,' she said, and tried to smile.

'That's it.' His fingers brushed the tears off her cheeks.

Lacey put her arms around him and shut her eyes. If she could only keep on holding him, feeling his strong body against her, the easy rise and fall of his chest, the gentle stroke of his hands on her back, then maybe nothing bad would happen.

The handle of his automatic felt flat and hard against Lacey's belly.

She might reach for it. But that would end the closeness, the trust. Better to keep that, to stay with him, than to risk losing it by going for the gun.

She felt another hardness, lower down.

Scott plucked the tails of her tank top from her shorts, and reached up inside it, caressing her back, then easing her away and moving gently to her breasts. He held them in each hand, his palms gliding against her turgid nipples. Lacey moaned. The hands continued to caress her for nearly a full second after she heard the crash of shattering glass.

Scott looked at her, stunned. 'The windows!'

CHAPTER EIGHTEEN

THE NOISE of the bursting window came from a distance, from the bathroom or bedroom. Lacey broke for the door. Dropping to a crouch, she grabbed her spray can and pocket knife. She glanced back. Scott was at the hallway entrance, pistol out.

'Let's run!' she snapped.

Scott glanced at her, frowning.

She kicked the chair. It dropped backwards to the floor, and she tugged the door open.

'Come on!'

Scott whirled around and ran. He scooped up a table leg and dashed after her through the door. He jerked it shut. 'Get ready. When he comes out, we'll . . .'

Lacey raced up the corridor. When she reached a corner, she looked back. Scott glanced from the door to her. She motioned for him. He muttered something through his teeth, then ran to join her.

'We had a chance . . .'

'We've got a better chance if he can't find us.' She shoved open a fire door.

They entered a dimly lighted stairwell. Scott thrust the door shut and leaned against it.

'Come on,' Lacey said. She started up the concrete stairs. 'He'll expect us to head down.'

'Where we going?'

'I don't know.' She turned at the first landing, and started up the next flight of stairs. Above her, she saw the blue metal door to the fourth floor. She raced up, Scott close behind her, and grabbed the knob. As she pushed the door open, Scott patted her arm. He pressed his forefinger to his lips. They stood motionless, listening.

For a moment, Lacey heard nothing. Then the metallic sound of a springing latch echoed quietly up the stairwell.

Scott shoved the door hard. It flew open, and he pointed to the upper steps. The door banged against the outside wall as they turned away and leapt up the stairs three at a time. In seconds, they reached the landing. Lacey charged up the remaining stairs. Halfway to the top, she heard the lower door clump shut.

Would it fool him? If so, he would only be delayed long enough to leave the stairwell and glance down the fourth floor corridor.

Scott, slightly above her, was first to reach the door. He held it open for Lacey. She raced through. Scott eased it shut, turning the knob to prevent the latch from snapping back into place.

With a few steps, they passed an ice machine and rounded a corner. Scott stopped, looking each way.

To the right, the corridor led past the doors of only half a dozen rooms, then abruptly ended. To the left, it seemed to stretch on forever.

'This way,' Scott muttered. He ran to the left.

Past rooms. Past a fire hose and ax. Past swinging doors of staff rooms.

Lacey, sprinting to stay beside him, saw a bank of elevators ahead. 'Let's try those,' she gasped.

They ran for them. The doors of all four elevators were shut. Scott threw himself against the nearest panel and jammed fingers into both buttons. Double disks of light appeared between each of the door sets: one with an arrow point up, the other down.

Lacey pressed herself to the wall beside him. Craning her neck, she gazed at the dark arrows above the doors. She gasped for air. The spray can and knife were slippery in her hands. She could feel the vibrations of the elevators against her back, hear the distant, quiet bells as they stopped at other floors. She looked up the corridor, squinting as if that might help her see the man's approach, then glanced again at the arrows above her. They stayed dark.

'This is no good,' she whispered.

With a nod of agreement, Scott flung himself away from the wall. They left the elevators behind and dashed down the corridor. Their feet thudded on the carpet. From behind came the quiet ding of an elevator bell. Lacey looked back. They were too far away to return in time. She ran hard to catch up with Scott.

Just ahead, a hallway led off to the left. Scott slowed and turned the corner. He stopped, and Lacey halted beside him. She leaned back against an ice machine, panting for breath.

'What now?' she gasped.

Scott pointed with the club in his left hand. A yard away was a fire door.

'Might as well.'

Across the hall, a door opened. A slight, young man in blue pajamas and a satin robe stepped out backwards. He pulled his door shut gently so it stopped against the frame. Turning around, he smiled a surprised greeting. In his hands, he held a cardboard ice bucket.

'Cheerio,' he said.

Scott lunged across the hall, grabbed the front of his robe, and thrust him into the room. Lacey followed. She shut the door quickly and silently.

'Hey now!' the man said. He seemed more offended than afraid. 'What . . .?'

Scott snarled and raised the club. The man's mouth snapped shut. He looked from Scott to Lacey, eyes narrowing behind his oversized glasses.

'We're Nick and Nora Charles,' Scott said. 'Asta's back in our room.'

'Oh?'

Scott let go of him. The man offered a small, pale hand. 'Hamlin Alexander.'

After shaking hands, they moved away from the door. One of the double beds was mussed, the other neatly made.

'You alone?' Scott asked.

'I just shooed away a nymphet. I don't expect her to return in the immediate future.' He set the ice bucket on the dresser beside a full bottle of Stolichnaya. 'Room service didn't provide ice. Expected me to fetch it myself, obviously. I don't suppose we might venture out for some, now that we're acquainted?'

'I don't think so,' Scott said.

'If you're indeed Nick and Nora, I doubt you intend to rob or mutilate me. Would you care for a warm drink?'

They nodded, and he opened the bottle.

'I don't suppose you caught my concert tonight? Really first-rate.'

'Sorry,' Scott said.

Hamlin poured vodka into three glasses. 'To a warm and *healthy* relationship,' he toasted.

Lacey sipped her vodka. Its strong taste made her cringe, but it felt warm and pleasant going down.

'Now,' said Hamlin. 'To what do I owe your presence? You're not a pair of lunatic fans, obviously. Am I a hostage of choice or opportunity?'

'Opportunity,' Scott told him. 'You came out your door at the right time.'

'The right time for you, perhaps.'

Though they were talking softly, Lacey worried that their voices might carry through the door. She crossed the room and turned on the television.

'Oh please,' Hamlin muttered. 'Ah, I see,' he said as Lacey increased the volume. 'Background noise. That's about all the cyclops is good for. Now, what brings you into my august presence?'

'We're being pursued by a killer.'

Hamlin raised his eyebrows, sat on his rumpled bed, and crossed his legs. 'I see you're well armed.'

'He has an Ingram, a small assault weapon capable of firing twenty rounds per second.'

'Nasty.'

'Extremely. So you can see that we'd prefer to avoid a

confrontation. If he didn't see us come in, we'll be all right. Even if he knows which floor we're on, I don't think he'll take the chance of barging into every room.'

'I hate to appear simplistic, but have you considered bringing in the gendarmes?'

'A special team is flying in from Washington,' Scott told him. 'We expect it to arrive,' he checked his watch, 'in roughly three, three and a quarter hours.'

'Washington? So we're embroiled in a cloak-and-dagger scheme? I should have guessed; you have that clean-cut, boy-next-door, FBI look about you.' He peered at Lacey as she sat down beside Scott on the other bed. 'Nora, however, is not an agent. No no. Too delicate, feminine, vulnerable. I should think Nora is an innocent bystander cast by mischance into the role of heroine.' He nodded shrewdly. 'Perhaps a witness?'

'Very observant,' Scott said.

'The fellow with the nasty weapon, a Ruskie agent?'

'Can't tell you.'

'The solution to your problem is make-up. I just happen to have, in my possession, an elaborate make-up kit complete with hair, teeth, blood, and Dick Smith's Flex-Flesh. I don't *just happen* to have it – very deliberate. I often travel incognito. For security and privacy, you understand. The kit has many uses, however. The nymphets blush and cream at the chance to be transformed into the monsters they are: zombies, hags with oozing pustules, vampires. The vampire is my specialty. Those sub-moronic sexpots throw themselves into the role with such abandon – snarling, baring their fangs – and it's rarely my neck they insist upon sucking. Quite delightful. I'd be more than happy to transform the two of you. Not into monsters, perhaps, but with a few deft touches and a change of clothes you might walk right past the murderous Ruskie without being recognized.'

'Thanks anyway,' Scott said.

'On the other hand, I might apply a multitude of wounds: bullet holes, slash marks, quantities of artificial blood. I'm

113

superb at corpses. I'll arrange you on the floor. If your maniacal Soviet should burst through the door, he'll assume you've already been dispatched. No need to repeat the process. *Voila!*'

'That's ridiculous,' Scott told him.

'It's genius. A subtle but profound difference.'

'Maybe. But I still think . . .' The deafening clamor of a bell in the corridor stopped his words.

Hamlin jumped, spilling his drink.

The high-pitched ringing went on.

'Fire alarm!' Scott shouted.

'You don't think . . .?'

Grabbing his makeshift club, Scott scurried off the bed and raced toward the door. Lacey picked up her spray can, her knife. Hurrying after him, she saw him touch the knob. 'Not warm,' he said. He looked back. 'Hamlin,' he yelled over the din. 'Get over here!'

The small man rushed to them. His face, so confident before, now looked drawn and pale.

'Look out the door. See if there's smoke.'

They stepped aside so they couldn't be viewed from the hallway, and Hamlin opened the door. 'Appears fine,' he said.

'Check around the corner.'

He stepped out. Scott held the door open a crack. A moment later, Hamlin shoved through it and gazed at them. 'Jesus H. Christ! The other end of the hall – all kinds of smoke. People spilling out of their rooms like . . . Christ, my horn!' He hurried past them. Seconds later, he returned with a black leather case. 'Don't know about you, but I'm getting the fuck out of here!' Flinging open the door, he dashed across the hallway to the fire door.

Lacey stepped out beside Scott. Half a dozen people were now in the short hall, most in night clothes, rushing for the door. Hamlin threw it open. He coughed as dark smoke bellowed into his face. He started to shut it, but the door knocked him backwards and a flaming man stumbled from the stairwell. His fiery arms reached for Hamlin, but the little man smashed them aside with his instrument case and leapt out of the way.

Screams mixed with the blaring alarm bells as the burning man staggered toward the onrushing group of guests. They scattered. Falling among them, he clutched the negligee of a horrified young woman. She lurched away, but flames were already starting to curl up her white gown. A nearby man ripped it from her shoulders. She kicked free of the garment and threw herself into his arms.

Scott grabbed Lacey's wrist. He jerked her after him, around the corner to the long corridor. Hamlin was far ahead of them, dashing through stunned guests, dodging some, stiff-arming others aside, the black case hugged under one arm like a football. Though the far end of the corridor was gray with rolling smoke, Lacey saw no flames.

'This way's blocked,' Scott yelled to an elderly couple heading toward them. The couple stopped, looking at each other with confusion as Scott and Lacey hurried by.

The greatest number of people was gathered in front of the elevator bank, screaming and shoving in a frenzy to get closer to the doors.

As Scott and Lacey reached the edge of the crowd, an elevator arrived. Its double doors slid open, but the small enclosure was already packed. A roar of protest bellowed from those inside as the mob pressed forward. Through a gap in the crowd, Lacey saw one of the men in the elevator jerked out. Amid darting fists, a new man took his place. The doors rolled halfway shut, then slid open again. A tiny, dark-haired man leapt high, clambering over the shoulders and heads of those inside, his right hand clasping a black leather case. A moment later, the doors closed.

'What'll we do?' Lacey asked.

'Forget the elev . . .'

A woman's shriek rose above the tumult. Lacey looked, couldn't see her, then saw the bloody head of a fire ax rise above the figures at the far side of the crowd. It swung down. The mob parted, people stumbling out of the way, yelling and screaming. The ax chopped down, knocking through the upraised arm of a man staggering backwards, and split his head. As he fell, the ax swung sideways, biting into the belly of a naked woman – the one whose nightgown had caught fire earlier.

Lacey gaped as the slaughter continued, the ax chopping from side to side, catching people in the chest and belly and throat. They fought and tripped over each other, trying to get away. For an instant, Lacey glimpsed the length of the weapon. It swung, held by no one – no one she could see. It hacked through a man's neck. His severed head tumbled through the air, spraying blood.

Lacey clutched Scott's arm. 'It's him!' she shouted.

'Come on!'

'Where?'

Side by side, they raced down the corridor. As they neared the corner, Lacey looked back. The ax had finished hacking its way through the mob. Splatters of blood hung suspended in the air behind it. Abruptly, it lurched forward.

Lacey gasped, and rounded the corner after Scott. He threw himself against the door of Hamlin's room – locked.

'Come on!'

They rushed farther down the short hall, leaping past the small fire spreading around the dead man like a pool of strange, burning blood.

The next door, too, was locked.

Only three remained. Scott glanced at them, apparently decided they would offer no more than this one, and drew out his automatic. He blasted a single shot through the area where the lock tongue entered the frame, and kicked the door open.

Lacey looked back.

The ax flew at her, flipping end over end.

Scott jerked her inside and slammed the door. He threw himself against it.

'Get a chair!' he yelled.

Lacey dashed across the room, grabbed a straight-backed chair from beneath the table, and ran with it to Scott. He braced it under the knob.

An instant later, the door thundered. An ax-head burst through it, high up, throwing out a shower of splinters.

'You're mine!' a man's voice cried out. 'Mine, cunt!'

The ax crashed again through the door, this time lower, smashing the chair down from the knob. The door flew open.

Gunfire shocked Lacey's ears, and she gazed at Scott. He was crouched and snarling, the automatic bucking in his grip as he fired shot after shot at the doorway.

Lacey covered her ears against the gun's endless roar.

The ax lunged forward, jerking in midair, and dropped to the floor.

CHAPTER NINETEEN

'SPRAY HIM,' Scott snapped as he braced the door shut.

Kneeling, Lacey aimed the paint can toward the ax. She pressed down the nozzle. A fine, silvery cloud sprayed out and drifted down, spreading into a layer half a foot above the carpet. As she moved the can back and forth, the surface took on features. She saw the heavily muscled, jutting slopes of shoulder blades, and realized she must be kneeling at his head. She gave it a quick blast. The paint misted his thick hair and sprayed cool against her own thighs. With a quick sweep to the right, she coated one of his arms. Then she sprayed the other. Its thick hand still gripped the haft of the ax.

Scott crouched and pried the fingers loose. He held the wrist. 'Still has a pulse,' he muttered. 'Hit lower, let's find the wounds.'

Lacey sprayed down the long, tapering expanse of his back. She hesitated at his waist, but only for a moment. Invisibility was his greatest weapon: painting him was like cutting Samson's hair. The hell with modesty. She sprayed his buttocks.

Then she took her finger off the nozzle and stared at his shiny back, at its three gaping, ragged wounds. Looking into them, she saw the green carpet several inches down. Clear, silver-dusted fluid overflowed the holes.

At the shoulder, she saw the crater of a healed gunshot wound. Near the center of his back was a narrow, inch-long ridge. The knife wound from Wednesday night? She touched it, feeling an edge of hardness. A scab? Her finger came away wet with paint. As she wiped it on her shorts, the fire alarm stopped blaring.

118

She looked at Scott. He shrugged.

In the quiet, she heard distant voices.

'Maybe it's out,' Scott said, his voice sounding odd in the stillness.

His hands moved from wound to wound. 'I missed the heart, thank God. Not much flow. If I didn't hit a major vessel . . .' He took off his shirt, and ripped its sleeves off. Folding one of the sleeves into a thick pad, he pressed it tightly to a wound near the side of the back. 'Hold it there,' he said. 'Hard.'

While Lacey kept the pad in place, he folded his other sleeve and pressed it to a second wound, lower down. Lacey held that one for him. He tore his shirt up the back, and used one of the halves to make another compress. He pushed it against the final wound.

'Right back,' he said. He hurried away and returned seconds later, holding a suitcase. He dropped it to the floor and threw it open. Crouching, he rummaged through it. He flung out a pair of pantie hose, a half-slip, several pairs of briefs. 'Those'll do,' he muttered. He took out a leather case, jerked open its zipper, and upended it. Out fell scissors, a plastic container of rubber bands and safety pins, a tiny sewing kit, a tube of Krazy Glue, a Swiss Army knife, and a roll of adhesive tape. 'Fantastic!' he blurted. He snapped open the metal cannister of tape.

Tearing off a strip, he tried to secure one of the bandages in place. The tape slid on the wet paint. Scott cursed under his breath, then grabbed the torn remnant of his shirt from the floor and swabbed the man's back, clearing off excess paint around the compresses until each was surrounded by no more than a vague, translucent stain. He tested the tape: it held.

Working together, Scott and Lacey quickly secured the pads to his back.

'Let's turn him.'

They rolled him onto his back.

'Don't paint him yet. I'll work by touch.' He picked up a pair of nylon briefs, scowled, and tossed them aside.

Then he pulled a cotton blouse from the suitcase and started to tear off its sleeves. As he folded them into pads, Lacey gazed down at the strange, sprawled shape of the man.

He looked like a legless, one-sided sculpture molded of aluminum foil. Circles of carpet were visible around his bandages. The unreality of the sight made Lacey nervous. 'I want to spray him,' she said. 'I'll stay away from the chest.'

Scott nodded. He bent over, a compress in one hand, reaching down with his other hand like a mime pretending to examine a make-believe patient.

Lacey aimed the paint can at the silver half-shell of the man's nearest arm, and sprayed. The paint wrapped over it, and the arm was suddenly human. Crawling past Scott, she sprayed the other arm. Then she scurried alongside the body. Using the concave globes of his rump as a guide, she sprayed the tops of both legs. Then she lifted them at the ankles and coated their undersides.

Scott was busy applying the final compress as Lacey shot spray from hip to hip, spreading a silver layer over the man's groin.

She stared at his penis. It lay to one side. Even flaccid, it looked thick and heavy, much larger than others she'd seen. No wonder it had felt so enormous inside her – ramming painfully, stretching her, making her bleed.

Disgusted, she looked away.

Scott met her eyes. 'Are you okay?' he asked.

'Yeah.'

Down the hall, someone knocked roughly on wood. 'Fire's out,' called a strong voice.

'Quick,' Scott said. 'Get the ax.'

Lacey picked it up. Scott grabbed the man's hands and raised his back off the floor. He dragged him away from the door. He pulled him around a corner of the room, and let him down alongside a wall. Then he took the ax from Lacey. He lifted a corner of the mattress, and hid the ax beneath it.

'Okay,' he said. 'Let's go see.'

'Just . . . leave him here?'

'Come on.' Scott slid his automatic under the bed, and hurried to the door. As they stepped into the smoky corridor, a policeman came out of the first room – Hamlin's room. He pivoted, bringing up his service revolver.

'Thank God you're here,' Scott blurted. 'Some maniac . . .'

'I know.' The cop holstered his pistol.

A fireman with a smudged face stepped out of the room.

'Came after us with a goddam ax,' Scott said. 'We were over by the elevators, and . . . Christ, did you see what he did to those people? He came after us – my wife and I . . .' Scott put an arm around Lacey. 'We barely got away. He tried to bash our door down.'

'What did he look like? Couldn't get a decent description from the others.'

The fireman walked past them, past their broken door, and knocked on the next door down. 'Fire's out,' he called. 'Anybody here?'

'Describe him,' the cop said. Glancing at the fireman, he called, 'Don't go in there without me.'

'Tall, maybe six-two. Long dark hair.'

'Caucasian?' the cop asked, writing on his note pad.

'Yes. Maybe thirty years old. He was wearing pajamas. Striped pajamas. Blue and white. I'm not sure, but I think he went out there.' Scott pointed at the fire door across from Hamlin's room. 'Didn't see him, but the door made a metal sound, you know, like it was closing.'

'ID?'

'Ours?' Scott asked.

'Please.'

Scott slipped a wallet from his hip pocket. He pulled out the driver's license and handed it to the officer.

'Name?'

'Scott Bradley.'

'This is your current address?'

'Yes.'

He copied the information, then returned the license. 'Thank you, Mr Bradley, missus. Now you two go on downstairs, see one of the officers in the lobby.'

'Can we get some things from the room?'

'Go ahead.' The policeman stepped past them.

Scott and Lacey entered the room. Scott shut the door.

'Now what?' Lacey asked.

'I don't know. I've got to think. They're clearing the building. We have to get him out of here, somehow.'

'Why don't we turn him over to the police?'

'Now? Are you joking? I've got to have a few hours alone with him.'

'But . . .'

'We could make a million bucks off the guy. Nobody's going to get a crack at him till I've had a chance to get his story.'

'If he dies . . .'

'Bite your tongue,' Scott said.

They stepped around the corner and Lacey looked down at the man. His chest and face were still unpainted. The chest bandages seemed to hang in space above his silver back.

'Okay,' Scott said. 'Let's leave him. We'll come back and pick him up later.'

Together, they pushed the body under the nearest bed. Scott retrieved his automatic. He shoved it into a front pocket, but the grips protruded. In the suitcase by the door, he found a pink bathrobe. He put it on and belted it. 'How do I look?'

The robe was much too small, his shoulders straining the fabric, the sleeves reaching only halfway down his forearms.

'Pink's your color,' Lacey said.

'We'd better make sure we get back here before the lady,' he muttered, and turned off the lights.

CHAPTER TWENTY

DUKANE BROUGHT his Cessna Bonanza in for a landing in Tucson, rented an Oldsmobile from Hertz, then sped toward the city.

He pressed a switch to lower the window, and put an arm out to catch the air. The night felt warm and dry.

Tuning in a country music station, he pressed the gas pedal to the floor. A straight, deserted road like this, no reason he shouldn't get it up to eighty. Cut off a few extra minutes. Might mean the difference to Scott.

Up against an invisible man? The more he thought about it, the crazier it sounded.

How the hell do you make a man invisible?

Even better, how do you nail him?

We shall see, Dukane thought, and began to sing along with Tom T Hall.

When he reached downtown Tucson, he knew there was too much commotion for 3 am. He swung the Olds onto Garfield Street. A block ahead of him, a fire truck and a dozen police cars filled the road. Their spinning domes flung red and blue lights over the crowd of onlookers, splashed their colors against walls and store windows. Most of the crowd's attention was focused on the hotel. The Desert Wind. Peering up through the windshield, Dukane saw no trace of fire or smoke. Except for a few broken windows, the hotel looked fine. Whatever had happened was over.

That explained why there was only a single fire truck. The others had already left. This one remained for the mop-up. Its crew might stay for a few hours, checking around, making sure the fire wasn't still burning secretly inside a wall, ready to blaze up the minute they took off.

But why all the police cars?

Easy. Because more must've happened than a fire.

He hadn't been in time to prevent it. From the look of things, whatever happened must've been an hour ago. At least. No way he could've arrived in time to help. Christ, he just hoped Scott was all right.

He turned the corner, and found an empty stretch of curb. He pulled over, took his attaché case from the back seat, and walked back to Garfield Street. Crossing to the left side, he made his way through the crowd. Many of the people were dressed in nightclothes, obviously hotel guests who'd been evacuated.

'What happened here?' he asked a man in a bathrobe.

'*Some* excitement, huh? Fire. And I hear some nut went after folks with an ax. Panicked, I guess. Killed half a dozen folks. I saw 'em cart out the bodies.'

'How long ago?'

'Seems like hours. All over, now. You should've got here sooner. Brought 'em out in body bags, just like in the news. All over, now. Hope they're gonna let us in pretty soon. Got a conference at nine. Can't very well go dressed like this, can I?'

Dukane shook his head, and moved on.

A hand clapped his shoulder from behind. He whirled around and looked into the haggard, boyish face of Scott.

'Glad you made it,' Scott said.

'Glad *you* did.'

'Dukane, this is Lacey Allen.'

She nodded a greeting. Her hair was mussed, her face dirty or bruised, the tail of her tank top half untucked.

'Let's go to my car,' he said. 'We can talk there.'

'So he's still in that room,' Scott finished, 'unless he walked off.'

'Or the police found him,' said Dukane.

'If they did, they haven't brought him out.'

'Not that we saw,' Lacey added, and stubbed out her cigarette in the car's ashtray.

'What'll we do?' Scott asked.

'If you're so determined to get his life story, I suppose we'll have to go up there and bring him out. Lacey, you'd better wait here. They'll have found the editor's body in your room. They'll be looking for you, and we can't have you pulled in for questioning just now. Scott, take off that silly robe.'

'But my Colt . . .'

'Leave it with Lacey.'

In the hotel lobby, Dukane showed a false FBI credential to the officer in charge, explaining he needed to retrieve paperwork from his room. He and Scott were allowed to pass.

As they stepped into an elevator, two men in plain clothes joined them. Dukane pushed a button for the fifth floor.

'Which floor?' he asked the men.

'Same.'

The door closed, and the elevator started upward.

'Are you gentlemen guests of the hotel?' asked the taller of the two. He was about forty, with neatly trimmed black hair and the weary, cynical eyes common to cops. He appeared in better shape than his younger buddy. From the thickness of his neck, Dukane guessed that he worked out with weights.

'We're on official business,' Dukane said.

'ID?'

Dukane showed it.

'FBI, huh? I'm impressed. Aren't we impressed, Arthur?'

'I know I am,' said Arthur.

'What about you?' he asked Scott.

'Me?' Grinning, Scott scratched his bare chest. 'I'm impressed, too.'

The man didn't look amused. 'Got an ID?'

'He's with me,' said Dukane.

The doors opened, and all four left the elevator. A uniformed cop nodded to the other pair. He glanced at Dukane and Scott.

'Let them pass,' said the tall one. 'FBI.' He pointed to a dark pool of blood. 'Try not to step in it.'

'We'll be careful,' Dukane said.

Scott nodded to the left.

'Hope you catch him,' Dukane told the men, and started away.

'We're not the FBI, but we sometimes do get our man.'

'I'm sure you do.'

'Come along, Arthur.' The pair turned to the right and started up the corridor.

Dukane and Scott walked the other way. As they reached the corner, Dukane glanced back. The uniformed cop was still near the elevator bank. The two in plain clothes had nearly arrived at the far end of the corridor.

'Lucky they didn't come with us,' Scott said.

'We're not out of here yet.'

Halfway up the short hall, Dukane spotted the battered door. He entered first, stepping over the strewn contents of a suitcase. Women's clothing.

Scott pointed to the first bed.

They crouched beside it. Dukane lifted the draping edge of the coverlet. In the space below the bed, he saw a naked, silver-skinned man. He grabbed an arm, and dragged the man out.

'Good Christ,' Dukane muttered, staring at the empty face, at the bandages suspended over the hollow chest cavity. He laid a hand on the chest. He felt the texture and warmth of skin where none was visible, felt the slow rise and fall of breathing. 'I'll be damned,' he said. 'I never would've believed it.'

'Thought I was kidding you?'

'Not exactly. Just figured you were mistaken, somehow. But he's invisible, all right.'

'How'll we get him out of here?'

'Won't be easy. Especially the way he looks.' Dukane swiped a finger over the paint. It was dry. 'Got any turpentine?'

Scott made a feeble laugh.

'Too bad he's not completely invisible when it would do us some good. Where's your room?'

'Third floor.'

'You still have the key?'

'Sure.'

'Go downstairs and bring up your luggage. You have extra clothes?'

Scott nodded.

'They'll be a tight fit on this guy, but we can't haul him out of here looking like this.'

'What about his face?'

'I don't know. Go get your stuff, though. Take the stairs. I don't want you running into more cops.'

Scott stood up. He started to turn away, but hesitated. 'You know, Matt . . . those cops. The plain clothes guys? They looked familiar to me. I can't quite place them, but . . .' He chewed his lower lip. 'They worry me.'

'Think about it. In the meantime, get your stuff up here.'

'Right.'

While Scott was gone, Dukane searched the suitcase of the room's occupant. He found no make-up, so he checked the bathroom. There, on a shelf above the sink, was a blue canvas satchel. He unsnapped it, folded it open, and studied the contents neatly arranged inside clear plastic pockets: cue tips, skin moisturizer, fingernail polish and remover, blush-on, mascara, lipstick, an eyebrow pencil, and a tiny tan bottle of make-up base. He took out the bottle of base, dabbed a bit of the fluid onto his fingertip, and tapped it on the mirror. The smudge was opaque, and nearly flesh colored. A bit too dark, with a reddish tinge, but close enough.

He took the bottle into the bedroom. Kneeling down, he poured the beige fluid onto the man's face and spread it evenly. The face took form under his fingers. He saw

127

the broad forehead, the prominent cheekbones, the hollow cheeks, the long narrow nose. As he progressed, he wished he had shaved the man. The make-up clung to his heavy eyebrows, gave his whiskers the look of spiky, mutated skin.

At the sound of footsteps, Dukane drew his automatic from its shoulder holster. Scott came in, swinging his suitcase and attaché case onto the bed.

'Any trouble?' Dukane asked.

'Didn't meet a soul. But I remembered about the cops. I saw them at dinner tonight.'

'Where?'

'At Carmen's, a couple of miles from here. They sat at a table across from us. Maybe it's just a coincidence . . .'

'A surveillance team.'

'Why would cops be watching Lacey and me?'

'Good question.'

Scott opened his suitcase. He tossed a sport coat, shirt, and a pair of trousers to the floor.

'Sunglasses?'

'Yeah.'

'We could use a hat.'

'He'd better not lose it,' Scott said, and removed a battered, tan fedora from his suitcase. He took out a shirt for himself. 'You did a nice job on his face.'

'If those cops were watching you, they might be showing up. Better watch the door. I'll dress our friend.'

Scott left.

Dukane slid the brown trousers up the man's legs, tugging to get them over his buttocks. They were a tight fit, but he managed to hook the waist shut. The bulky, silver privates still hung outside the fly. Dukane hesitated, reluctant to touch them. Holding his breath as if he were handling excrement, he tucked the scrotum into the pants, then pushed the penis inside. As he started to withdraw his hand, silver fingers grabbed it and pressed it to the soft flesh.

Dukane jerked his hand away.

The man chuckled.

Backing off, Dukane drew the automatic from his shoulder holster.

'You don't need that,' said a quiet, raspy voice. 'I'm going with you guys.'

'Explain.'

'I been listening. Don't know who you are, but you're not with The Group. You get me out of here, protect me, I won't give you no trouble. I'll do whatever you want. You name it. Just don't let the others take me.'

'A deal,' he said, but didn't lower the gun. 'How are you feeling?'

'Like I got the shit kicked out of me. I been shot before, only not this bad.'

'Those wounds should've killed you.'

'Not me, man. I'm Sammy Hoffman, Wonder Man. Takes more than a few fuckin' bullets to switch me off.'

'Can you sit up?'

Grimacing, he pushed himself off the floor. He raised his arms in front of his face, and turned them. 'Fuck, man, I look like the Tin Woodsman.'

'Put on this shirt.'

He took it. 'Where's my pal, Lacey?'

'Waiting outside.'

'She going with us?'

'Yes.'

'Oh good.' He drew the shirt taut across his chest and buttoned it. Dukane gave him the sport coat. 'You guys gonna try and walk me out of here?'

'That's the idea.' He found a pair of socks in Scott's suitcase, and tossed them to Hoffman.

'Those bastards from the Group'll give us trouble.'

'We'll handle it.'

'Man, you better. They want my ass.' He finished putting on the socks.

'Put your hands on top of your head.'

'Hey, come on.'

'Do it,' Dukane said, and tugged handcuffs out of his

rear pocket. He stepped behind Hoffman, pulled one arm down behind him, cuffed it, then brought down the other arm and snapped the second bracelet around its wrist.

He put the sunglasses on Hoffman's face, concealing the empty eye sockets. Then he placed Scott's old fedora on the man's head. 'Okay, on your feet.'

Hoffman stood up.

Dukane led him to the door, where Scott was crouched and peering through the ax holes.

'Any sign of our friends?'

'Looks clear.' Scott turned, glanced at Hoffman, and wrinkled his nose. 'He doesn't look like much.'

'It's the best I can do. He'll pass, as long as nobody gets a close look.'

'Long as they're a mile off.'

'Better leave your luggage here.'

'Gotta bring my galleys. And recorder.' He hurried away, and returned a few seconds later with his attaché case.

They left the room, Dukane holding Hoffman's right arm, Scott his left. Dukane shoved open the fire door.

Two revolvers pointed at his chest. Two men grinned.

'Greetings,' said the taller one. 'Come in, come in. Don't just stand there.'

They stepped onto the landing.

'Well Arthur, looks like the FBI got their man – *our* man. Tough rocks, Sammy. That *is* you, I take it.'

'Go fuck yourself, Trankus.'

'You're not an easy guy to catch. I must thank you fellows, and of course Miss Allen, for being of such invaluable assistance.'

'Glad to help,' Dukane said. He glanced at Scott. 'Don't try anything.'

Scott nodded.

Arthur frisked him, taking his knife. Then he took away Dukane's automatic and switchblade.

'Very good,' said Trankus.

'Glad to cooperate with the police.'

'Now, let me lay out our alternatives. Arthur and I are, of course, bone fide members of the Tucson Police Department. As such, we'll be able to walk you three gentlemen out of the hotel, no questions asked. We will then transport you to the destination of our choice.'

'Not the police station, I assume.'

'True. You're a bright fellow, probably not FBI at all.'

'Just a regular guy.'

'Valuable catches, all three of you. Wonderful bonuses for us, if we deliver you intact. On the other hand, Sammy is top priority. You two are quite expendable, whoever you are. Therefore, if you make any attempt to resist us, we shall cheerfully expend you. Right now, if you prefer.'

'We won't resist,' Dukane said.

'Excellent. You two hold onto Sammy, and precede us down the stairs. When we reach the lobby, we'll leave by the main door.'

'Whatever you say.'

Keeping their grips on Hoffman, they started down the stairs.

'You fuckers aren't gonna let these guys have me?' he whispered.

'We don't have much choice.'

'You're nuts. You don't know what they'll do to you. You never been questioned by The Group, man. They'll stick an electric wire up your dick . . .'

'Knock it off,' Trankus said.

'You guys are better off shot dead here on the stairs. I'm telling you . . .'

'Where there's life, there's hope,' said Trankus.

'Not if they get you to the compound.'

'Compound?' asked Dukane. 'What's that?'

'Get me out of here, and I'll take you. A guided fuckin' tour.'

'You always did have stupid ideas,' Trankus said. 'That's what got you into this mess. How could you have *imagined* you'd get away with it?'

'Done all right, till now.'

131

'Certainly. Our people have been following your progress, Sammy. For an invisible man, you left a wonderfully visible trail. A word of advice, though it's a bit late – always conduct your affairs in such a way as to stay out of the news.'

'Thanks.'

They reached the door to the lobby. 'Stop,' Trankus said. He stepped past them, and pushed open the door.

They drew curious glances as they crossed the lobby. 'Looters,' Trankus explained. That seemed to satisfy the other cops.

In seconds, they were outside.

'What about Lacey?' Dukane asked.

'For Christsake!' Scott snapped.

'Oh, we wouldn't forget Miss Allen.' When they reached the sidestreet, Trankus said, 'This way.' Apparently, he knew just where to find the car.

They walked up the center of the deserted street.

As they neared the car, Dukane saw Lacey watching through a window. He raised a hand as if to scratch his belly, made a fist with his forefinger protruding and worked his thumb up and down.

They reached the car.

'Miss Allen, would you care to join us?' Trankus pressed the muzzle of his revolver against Dukane's ear.

Dukane nodded.

Lacey swung open the driver's door. She held Scott's automatic at her waist.

Dukane threw his arm up, knocking Trankus's pistol back. The blast deafened him, scorched the nape of his neck. A second blast, from the car, caught Trankus in the chest.

Arthur crouched and aimed at Lacey.

Hoffman started to run.

Scott swung his attaché case, smashing aside Arthur's pistol.

Dukane tripped Hoffman. As the man tumbled to the street, Scott drove two fingers into Arthur's eyes, then

132

chopped his throat. Grabbing Trankus's gun off the pavement, Dukane put a bullet into Arthur's head.

They retrieved the other weapons.

Then they dragged Hoffman to the car and flung him into the back seat. Dukane climbed in on top of him. Scott shoved Lacey into the passenger seat, and the car sped away.

CHAPTER TWENTY-ONE

LACEY SAT huddled against the passenger door, shaking as her mind replayed the kick of the pistol, the stunned look on the man's face when her bullet slammed into him, the way he flopped backwards with his hands groping the air. She told herself it was necessary, she *had* to shoot him. That didn't help. She felt cold and sick.

At first, the car hurled up the street, skidded around a corner, then around another corner. Lacey held tightly to the door handle as the momentum tugged at her.

Then the car slowed to a moderate speed.

'Looks all right behind,' Dukane said.

'Where to?'

'The desert?'

'Which way?'

'This way's fine. I'll tell you when to turn.'

Scott nodded, then looked over at Lacey. 'How are you doing?'

'Rotten.'

'You did great.'

'Who . . . who were they?'

'Apparently from some group that's after Hoffman.'

'Hoffman?'

'Our invisible friend,' Scott said. 'His name is Samuel Hoffman.'

'Elsie's son?'

'That's right,' Hoffman muttered.

'My God! He did that . . . butchered her that way? His own mother?'

'She was a cunt,' came the rough voice from the back seat. 'Same as you.'

'Shut up,' snapped Dukane.

Turning, Lacey looked around at the man beside Dukane. The hat was gone. So were the sunglasses. The eyeless blur of face looked grotesque and unfamiliar, more like a death's head than the face of Sammy Hoffman. She quickly turned away.

She hadn't seen Sammy in nearly ten years, not since the day he attacked Miss Jones. But she remembered the way he always stared at her. Sometimes, he even followed her.

Then came the night in her bedroom. She always liked to open the curtains, after getting into her nightgown, so the sun would fill her room in the morning. This time, when she opened them, she found a monster staring up at her, its nose and cheek mashed crooked against the window screen. She screamed. The hideous face lurched back, its features returning to normal, and she recognized Sammy. 'You creep!' she shrieked as he dashed away. 'You god-damn creep!'

Her father phoned Sammy's parents, that night. They were furious, said they would make Sammy wish he'd never been born. They must have carried out their threat, too; the next morning, Sammy showed up in class with a black eye and welts on his arms.

That was the day he attacked Miss Jones. Lacey never heard for sure, but rumor claimed that he raped the young teacher. Afterward, Lacey felt sick when she thought about it. Had she been to blame, somehow? It only made her feel worse to realize how glad she was that Sammy had chosen the teacher to rape, not her.

Well, he'd got her at last. Over and over again. She pressed her thighs tightly together, as if to prevent him from getting between them once more.

Looking out the windshield, she saw that they had left the city behind. The desert road was dark except for a half-moon and the bright tunnel of the headlights. Off to the sides, the terrain looked bleak and rugged. Saguaro cacti stood in the distance like lonely, disfigured men

135

watching them pass. Occasionally, she saw a house. They were few and dark.

She wished she were home and safe, and Sammy Hoffman far away, locked up where he could never get at her again. Locked up or dead.

'Make a left here,' Dukane said.

Slowing the car, Scott turned onto a narrow, two-lane road.

'We'll find a place to hole up, get your friend's story.'

'Gonna write me up?' Hoffman asked.

'Lacey and I,' Scott said, 'want to write a book about you. We want to get your whole story on tape.'

'Don't waste your time. Laveda, she'll see you never live to do it.'

'Laveda?' Dukane asked, sounding shocked. 'She's mixed up in this?'

'Mixed up? Hell, she's it. She's behind the whole fuckin' thing. And you're all on her list, now. They know you've been with me. They've gotta shut you up. Too bad, huh Lacey? I hate to see good quiff get wasted.'

Lacey heard Hoffman grunt.

'Just pointing out the facts of life.'

Scott glanced at Lacey. 'You'll be okay. We'll take care of you.'

'Is he right, though? Will they try to kill us?'

'They won't get us,' Dukane said.

'What's to stop them?'

'Me and Scott.'

'I'm glad *you're* so confident,' Lacey said.

'If necessary, we'll set ourselves up with new identities.'

'I don't think I'd like that,' she said, and stared out the window. A new identity. No more Lacey Allen, no more Oasis. Life in a strange town, always afraid the truth will be uncovered and the hunters will come. On the other hand, she no longer had strong ties to Oasis. After her parents were killed in a car crash, she'd simply stayed on because the town was familiar and comfortable. Most of her childhood friends had moved on. The job at the *Tri-*

bune was pleasant and secure, but she'd often felt restless, had thought of heading out for a more challenging job in LA, or San Francisco. Only inertia held her back. Why abandon the safe, routine life of Oasis for the unknown? Someday, maybe. Someday she would just up and leave. Alone, if she had to. But she always imagined a man would come along, one day, and take her hand, and lead her into a new life.

The man, apparently, was Sammy Hoffman. But he didn't lead her into a new life, he dragged her screaming.

She wished for the old security, the peace she'd known before he came along. But it was gone forever. She'd been terrorized, beaten and raped, she'd seen people butchered, she'd killed a man herself, and now she was faced with a life of hiding.

She suddenly realized, with a mixture of regret and excitement, that she had already lost Lacey Allen. Lacey had died, had been reborn into a new and horrible world. No longer the same person, she deserved a new name.

A natural step, when the rest of your identity has changed so completely. Maybe the new Lacey, whatever her name might be, would make a better life for herself. The old one hadn't done so well, not really. This was a chance to abandon her old ways, to seek out what she had missed.

'Might not be so bad,' she said.

'What?' Scott asked.

'Starting over.'

'Better than the alternative,' said Dukane.

'Don't worry about it, Lacey.'

'She better worry about it,' Hoffman said. 'You all better. Only way I stayed alive, this long, is 'cause I'm invisible.'

'There is another solution,' Dukane said.

'Yeah? I'd like to hear it.'

'Kill Laveda.'

Hoffman made a single, husky laugh. 'Sure thing. You saw how easy it is to kill me? All those fuckin' bullets and

137

here I am, like nothing happened? Well, Laveda made me that way. And next to her, I'm nothing. I bet I don't have a tenth of her powers. You're crazy if you think you can kill . . .'

'Damn,' Dukane muttered. 'There's a car behind us. No headlights. About half a mile back.'

'How long's it been there?'

'I just spotted it. The moon caught its windshield, I think. Could've been on our tail since Tucson.'

'I thought you said we were clear.'

'Thought we were.'

Looking over her shoulder, Lacey glanced at the grotesque, eyeless face of Hoffman and felt the back of her neck prickle. She quickly turned her attention to the rear window. She saw the red glow of their own tail lights, the pale moonlit strip of road, but no other car. 'I don't see it,' she said.

'It's there.'

'Police?' Scott asked.

'Cops wouldn't run blind.'

'You guys gotta do something,' Hoffman said. He sounded scared. 'They got us spotted, they'll start coming out of the fuckin' woodwork.'

'Not much woodwork around here,' Dukane said.

'You got no idea, man. No idea. You think we've got guys in the cops, we've got 'em *everywhere*. Every fuckin' corner of the country. Man, I'm top priority. There ain't nothing they won't do to nail my ass. They'll swarm us. We'll be dead meat in an hour.'

'Calm down.'

'You gotta get this *paint* off me!'

'Shut up. Scott, cut the lights as we round this bend, then swing off the road. See if we can't lose 'em.'

As the headlights died, Lacey faced front and grabbed her door handle. The car swerved to the left and sped off the road, lurching over the rough ground, slamming down a cactus that stood in the way like a man with upraised arms, bounding over hillocks and landing hard, finally careening down the steep side of a gully. Lacey threw a hand against the dash as the car slid to a stop.

'Watch Hoffman,' Dukane said, and leapt from the car.

'I ain't going nowhere.'

Lacey saw Dukane scramble to the top of the gully and sprawl flat. She opened the glove compartment. With trembling hands, she took out a cigarette and lit it. She inhaled deeply, held the smoke inside, and slowly blew it out.

Hoffman coughed. 'Bad for your health,' he said. Then he laughed softly. 'Not that it matters. None of us gonna live long enough for cancer.'

'Shut up,' Scott said.

She was nearly down to the filter by the time Dukane returned.

'It went by,' he said through the window.

'It'll be back,' said Hoffman. 'The fuckers are psychic.'

Ignoring him, Dukane stepped to the front of the car and crouched down. 'Oh shit,' he muttered. 'I thought so. Broken axle.'

'What'll we do?' Scott asked.

'Walk.'

CHAPTER TWENTY-TWO

THEY TRAVELED parallel to the road, well away from it so they wouldn't be spotted if a car should pass. They only saw the road, themselves, when they sometimes reached higher ground.

Scott carried both attaché cases. Dukane, pistol in hand, walked behind Hoffman. Lacey stayed close to Scott, her eyes on the rough ground.

A long time had passed since Lacey's last hike in the desert. She remembered that time clearly. She was with Brian. They left his car by the road, and walked for nearly an hour in the fresh warmth of early morning. He took photos with his Polaroid: of cacti, of wild flowers, of lizards, of Lacey. They drank wine and ate cheese. The heat and alcohol made her tipsy. When she got tipsy, she got horny. They stripped and took pictures of each other, and that turned her on even more, and finally they spread their clothes on the burning ground and made love.

She looked at Scott, walking slightly ahead and to her right. His shirt clung to his back with sweat. His wallet made a bulge over his left buttock. She remembered the feel of him during those seconds when they embraced in the hotel room. If only they hadn't been interrupted . . .

Three years, now, since she'd taken a man in her arms, into her body.

Except for Hoffman.

He doesn't count.

She felt his hardness plundering her, and her excitement turned into an icy knot of revulsion. She watched him walking beside Dukane, the back of his head silver in the moonlight, his hands cuffed behind him. He looked undamaged. Why hadn't the bullets killed him, damn it? She should've grabbed Scott's gun, when they had him down, and pumped a few rounds into his head.

Maybe she still could.

But that would end Scott's dream of a bestseller.

Besides, she didn't know if she could kill another person – even Hoffman. The look on that man's face when her bullet hit him . . .

A dead saguaro lay at her feet like a rotting corpse. She stepped over it.

'Ah ha!' Dukane said, and pointed.

On a distant rise of land stood a small house. Its windows were dark, its stone walls pale. A pickup truck stood in front of it.

'The gods are smiling on us,' Scott said.

Lacey guessed the house was half a mile away, and set far back from the road – far enough, she hoped, so that it hadn't been noticed by those in the other car. Of course, they must've seen its entry drive. Maybe they'd already checked the place and moved on.

The house vanished as she made her way down the side of a gully.

Hoffman grunted. He stumbled, fell headlong, and tumbled to the bottom. 'Shit!' he snapped, rolling onto his back. 'Fuckin' handcuffs!'

Dukane pulled him to his feet.

'Get these things off me, 'fore I kill myself.'

'That's hardly likely.'

'Damn it, take 'em off! What do you think I'll do, run for it? Where'll I go? I'm with you guys, now. You're my only chance. I wouldn't break for it if I could, not with The Group on our fuckin' tails. I'm yours. Get me some-place safe. Man, those bastards are gonna roast me. Just let me have my hands so I don't bust my damn neck. That asking too much? I ain't gonna be any good to you guys with a busted neck.'

Dukane took a key from his pocket.

'Don't,' Lacey warned.

'We'll cuff him in front.'

'No! For Christsake, he'll get loose!'

'It's risky,' Scott said. 'He's stronger than you'd think.'

'Okay. I'll lay down. How's that?' Hoffman asked, dropping to his knees. 'Can't run if I'm lying down, right?' He fell forward, landing on his side, and rolled to his belly. 'Just put the cuffs in front. That'll be okay. You oughta try walking in this fuckin' desert with your hands behind your back, see how you like it.'

Dukane crouched over him.

'Wait!' Lacey said. 'Maybe he tripped on purpose. Just so he'd have an excuse for you to take off the cuffs.'

'Shut the fuck up,' Hoffman snapped.

'He didn't have much trouble before. Now, when we're in easy shot of a pickup truck, he suddenly can't stay on his feet.'

'Stupid cunt.'

'Lacey's right,' Scott said.

'Yeah. Okay, up.'

'Up *yours*. I'm not taking one more step till you change the cuffs. You want to drag me? Go ahead. Have fun.'

'What happened to your spirit of cooperation?' Dukane asked.

'You can fuckin' carry me.'

'Is that your last word on the subject?'

'Damn right.'

'Sorry to hear that.' Dukane stepped close to Hoffman's head.

'Are we gonna carry him?' Scott asked.

'I think he'll decide to walk.'

'Think again, asshole.'

Dukane stomped on his head, smashing his face into the gravel floor of the gully. Lacey cringed, shocked by the sudden violence. As she turned away, Scott took her into his arms. She pressed her face to his chest. Behind her, Hoffman's yell of pain became hysterical gasping.

'You . . . you . . . oh you bastard! I'll kill you, I'll kill you!'

142

'You'll walk with us,' Dukane said, his voice quiet and calm.

'I'll tear out your heart, you motherfuckin' . . .'

Lacey heard a thud, a grunt.

'You . . .!'

'Time to go,' Dukane said. 'You won't like it, if I lose my patience.'

'It's all right,' Scott whispered. He eased Lacey away, and she saw Dukane jerking the man to his feet.

'My *face!*'

'Not much loss, Hoffman. Nobody can see it, anyway.'

Hoffman turned to Lacey. She stared at his moonlit face, its eyeless sockets, its snarling mouth, gaps in its forehead and left cheek where the make-up or skin had been scraped off, a few patches of tinted flesh hanging like torn cloth. 'Your fault,' he told her. 'I'll get you for this.'

'You'll get no one,' Dukane said, and shoved him toward the slope.

They climbed out of the gully. The house seemed no closer than before. Lacey wondered if its occupants had heard Hoffman's outcries. Noise carries far in the desert, just as it does over water. But the windows were still dark. Perhaps the walls of the gully had contained most of the sound. Or maybe those in the house were heavy sleepers.

Lacey hoped the house was deserted. That seemed unlikely, though, with a pickup parked in front.

Along the way, Hoffman fell several more times as if to prove his point. Each time, he cursed the handcuffs that stopped him from catching himself. But he didn't stay long on the ground. He struggled quickly to his feet, looking around at Dukane.

Finally, they made their way up the low hill to the house. They took a path through the cactus garden at its side.

'Give me your shirt, Scott.'

Without hesitation, Scott took off his shirt and handed it over. Dukane draped it over Hoffman's head and used his own belt to cinch it around the neck.

'Want me to go around back?' Scott asked.

Dukane shook his head. 'Let's play it straight.' Holstering his pistol, he took Hoffman's elbow and led the way to the front door. He pressed the doorbell. From inside the house came a quiet ring of chimes.

They waited.

He rang again.

A light came on above the door.

'State your business,' called a voice from inside – the voice of a young woman.

'Our car broke down,' Dukane said. 'We'd like to use your phone.'

'I don't have one. Go on, get out of here.'

'We're worn out,' Lacey said. 'At least let us have some water. We've been walking a long time.'

'Use the tap by the garden,' she called. 'You're not getting in here. I saw you coming. You've got guns.'

'We're FBI, ma'am,' Dukane told her.

'Sure. And I'm John Edgar Hoover.'

'She hasn't got a phone anyway,' Lacey whispered.

'Okay, Scott. Get over there and hotwire the pickup.'

With a nod, Scott turned away.

'All right, lady,' Dukane said. 'We'll leave.'

'That's just fine.'

Lacey turned to follow Scott, and grabbed his arm as a woman with a double barreled shotgun lurched upright in the pickup's bed.

'No you *don't*!' yelled the woman.

CHAPTER TWENTY-THREE

THE FRONT door swung open. A woman stepped out with a revolver. She was slim, no older than twenty, with black hair cropped short. Though she must have had plenty of time to dress, she wore only a short pink nightgown. Apparently, thought Lacey, she'd been determined to keep them out.

'Put down your guns,' she said.

Dukane nodded to Scott. They set a total of four pistols on the ground: two of their own, plus the two they'd taken from Trankus and his partner.

'They were planning to make off with the truck,' said the other woman, climbing down. 'Otherwise, I would've let them go.' She was larger than the one in the doorway, with broad hips, and breasts that swung loosely inside her T-shirt.

'What'll we do?' asked the smaller one.

'Let's get them inside and call the police.'

'You *do* have a phone,' Dukane said.

'Of course.'

'Okay, inside.'

The small one backed into the house, waving her revolver. The one with the shotgun took up the rear. When they were all inside, she shut the door.

'Okay, Nancy, call the cops.'

'Don't do that,' Dukane said. 'Here, look at my credentials.' He handed his wallet to the girl with the pistol.

She slipped it open and stared. 'Says he's FBI, Jan.'

'Anybody can get a fake ID.'

'We were escorting our prisoner to Tucson when our car broke down.'

145

'What's he doing with a shirt on his head?' Jan asked.

'He's deformed,' Dukane explained. 'We put the shirt over him to spare you the sight.'

'Bullshit,' Jan said.

'It's true,' Lacey told her.

'They covered my head 'cause they kidnapped me and don't want you seeing who they've got. They snatched me this morning. I'm Watson Jones, vice president for Wells Fargo . . .'

'Can it, Hoffman.'

'Let him talk,' said Jan.

'They're holding me for two million bucks. The three of 'em, they're in it together. Look, get these cuffs off me, huh? Dukane, he's got a key.'

'Heard about a kidnapping?' Jan asked Nancy.

'No.'

'They ain't released it to the news.'

With relief, Lacey saw a wry smile on Jan's face.

'For the vice president of a bank, buster, you ain't got such good grammar.'

'He's a rapist and murderer,' Dukane said.

'That's a con! Get his fuckin' key before he grabs your guns.'

'Nobody's going to grab your guns,' Dukane said. 'This is your house. Fine with us if you want to hold the artillery. As I said before, we just want the use of your telephone. I need to call headquarters so they can pick us up.'

'We'd better call the cops. Nancy?'

'You don't want to do that,' Dukane said.

'Yes, I think we do.'

Nancy walked backwards across the red ceramic tile of the living room, and lowered herself onto a couch. She reached out for a telephone on the lamp table.

'Where'd she go?' Hoffman blurted. 'What's she doing? Don't let her call!'

'If you make that call,' Dukane said, 'it's quite possible we'll all be dead by morning.'

Nancy looked at Jan.

146

'Explain yourself,' Jan said.

'Our friend here belongs to a certain organization – a cult that wants him back. They have connections inside the Tucson police.'

'Suppose we call the Highway Patrol?'

'They may or may not be infiltrated. I don't know about that. But I do know this: if you phone in, they'll dispatch a car to this location by radio. Any joker with a Bearcat scanner will know right where to find us.'

'We'll be dead meat,' Hoffman said.

'What do you think?' Jan asked her friend.

Nancy shook her head, looking confused.

'It's all too damned fishy for me. Go ahead and call the Highway Patrol.'

'Don't,' Dukane warned.

Nancy lifted the receiver and dialed for the operator. 'Hello? I'd like the number . . .'

'Please,' Lacey said, starting forward. 'Put it down.'

Jan swung the shotgun toward her. At that instant, Dukane leapt. He caught Jan around the hips, throwing her backwards. The shotgun fired.

As its roar stunned Lacey's ears, she saw the base of the phone jump from the table, exploding, crashing into the lamp behind it. Phone and lamp flew against the blasted wall. Dukane and Jan hit the floor.

Scott rushed Nancy. The girl, frozen by the blast that barely missed her, offered no resistance. She sat on the couch, phone receiver still in her right hand, gazing at the splintered table surface as Scott freed the pistol from her left hand.

'What happened?' Hoffman yelled. 'Somebody take this fuckin' shirt off my head! Who got shot?'

Dukane, on top of Jan, shoved the shotgun across the floor. She stopped struggling. As he pinned her arms, they both gazed toward Nancy.

'She's okay,' Dukane said.

'Get off me,' Jan muttered.

He climbed off, and went for the shotgun. Jan hurried

to the couch. She sat down and put an arm around the girl. 'I'm sorry,' she said. 'I almost . . .' She began to cry. The daze left Nancy's face. Her chin trembled, and she lay her head against Jan's breast.

'Why don't you all just get out of here,' Jan blurted. 'Get the hell out. Take the pickup. Just get out of here.'

'Where are the keys?' Dukane asked, his voice gentle.

'My purse. In the kitchen.'

He went for them, and returned a moment later. 'I'll see that the truck's returned to you,' he said.

'Just get out.'

'Come on,' he said.

They went outside, leaving the two women on the couch. Dukane lowered the tailgate. He and Scott lifted Hoffman onto the truck bed. 'I'll ride in the back with him,' he said, climbing aboard with the shotgun.

They closed the tailgate. Scott lifted the two attaché cases over the side panel. He took the pistols off the ground, and gave two of them to Dukane.

'You take this,' he said, handing Nancy's revolver to Lacey.

They climbed into the cab.

As Scott started the truck, Lacey saw Jan gazing out one of the front windows of the house.

'They'll be all right,' Scott said.

'Now that we're gone.'

'Yeah.' He pulled the truck away from the house, with the headlights off, and sped up the long, narrow road. The deep blue of the sky was lighter in the east. Lacey wondered at it, for a moment, then realized the night was nearly over.

She leaned back and shut her eyes. She felt weary and sick, but not sleepy. Taking a deep breath, she was nearly overcome by nausea. Her mind whirled with images of Nancy's shocked face, the face of the man she had shot, the screams as Hoffman chopped through the crowd at the elevators, little Hamlin Alexander leaping into the packed elevator, the knife plunging into Carl's throat. She snapped open her eyes. 'Oh God,' she muttered.

'It'll soon be over.' Scott patted her leg.

'All this death . . .'

'I know.'

And then she saw a dark car ahead of them on the road, its doors open, men crouched behind the doors with guns.

'Down!' Scott yelled, and hit the brakes.

CHAPTER TWENTY-FOUR

LACEY FLUNG herself sideways as the night exploded. Scott dropped in front of her, his back striking her nose, shoving at her breasts. Dazed, she wondered if he'd been hit. But she felt him moving. Then the truck lurched backwards. It gained speed. The rear end swerved and she felt the truck bound off the smoothness of the road. It rose. It pounded down. Through the gunfire and roar of the engine, she heard rapid thunks like a dozen hammers pounding metal. The tail of the truck swung back. She felt the smoothness again.

Raising her head, she saw the blasted windshield and Scott's hand gripping the side of the steering wheel. As she looked, a bullet blasted through the top of the wheel. She ducked again.

The truck sped wildly, bumped off the other side of the road, swerved back, stayed on the pavement for a while, then lurched off again.

The shooting stopped. She felt Scott raise himself slightly, perhaps enough to peer out. Then he moved higher. He sat up. Lacey lifted her head. The road had turned. The other car was out of sight.

Scott floored the gas pedal.

'You okay?' he asked.

'Yeah.' Sitting up, she realized her nose was bleeding. She licked the blood from her upper lip, wiped it with the back of her hand.

The truck skidded to a stop. They were in front of the house again. Looking down the road, Lacey saw no sign of the car. She jumped from the cab and followed Scott to

150

the house. He unlocked the door. Stepping inside, she scanned the living room. Deserted.

She returned to the truck and grabbed the attaché cases while Scott and Dukane hustled Hoffman to the ground. He fell. As Dukane stood over him, Scott climbed into the pickup. Lacey watched him drive the smoking vehicle along the front of the house and through the cactus garden. At the edge of the slope, he jumped clear. The pickup plunged down. She heard it bang and slam. She expected it to explode, but it didn't.

'Why'd he do that?' she asked Dukane.

'The truck's no good. Too shot up. No point giving the bastards any extra cover.'

'At least we don't have the ladies to contend with,' Scott said as he returned. 'They high-tailed it. I saw 'em out there, running like a couple of jack rabbits.'

'They're best out of it,' Dukane said.

He and Dukane grabbed Hoffman and dragged him into the house. Lacey shut the door, locked it.

'Get the lights,' Dukane said.

Lacey switched off the outside light, then stepped to the near end of the couch and turned off the remaining lamp. Darkness filled the room.

'Watch out the window, Lacey. Scott, give me a hand. We'd better secure our friend.'

They pulled Hoffman to his feet and led him out of the living room.

Moving a rocker away, Lacey knelt at a front window. The road was deserted. In the east, the sky was a pale blue. She took a deep, shaky breath, and touched the skin beneath her nostrils. The bleeding had stopped. She folded her arms on the window sill, and rested her chin on her hands.

She thought of Jan and Nancy running through the desert, and wished she were with them. Running. Leaving all this behind. But she couldn't leave Scott. She would stick this out with him, see it through to the end.

She thought of the old movie, *Bonnie and Clyde* – the

ambush, bullets ripping into Warren Beattie and Faye Dunaway, making their bodies dance and writhe as if in a horrible orgasm.

Maybe it wouldn't hurt so much. You must go into shock right away. And then it's over.

The glow of the sun reached over the horizon, casting gold across the desert. She lay her forehead down on her folded hands, and wept.

'It's all right,' said a voice behind her. Scott's voice. His hands slipped under her armpits, and he lifted her. He turned her around to face him. 'It's all right,' he said, more softly. His fingertips brushed tears from her cheeks.

'I don't want us to die.'

' "We owe God a death," as Falstaff says.' He kissed her. 'But it's not due yet.'

She put her arms around him, and held him tightly. She pressed her face to the warm curve of his neck. He rubbed her back, her shoulders. Then he eased her away and led her past Dukane.

'I'll tuck her in,' he said.

Dukane nodded.

Scott guided her to a bed of cushions and blankets prepared in a short hallway. The nearby doors were closed.

'Where's Hoffman?' Lacey whispered.

'The bathroom. We cuffed him to the base of the sink. He can't get loose.'

'Can we use the bedroom?'

'Safer here. No windows.'

He lay down beside her, and held her gently.

Closing her eyes, Lacey felt his mouth on her open lips. His hand stroked her belly and slowly, so slowly, inched upward. Fingers glided over her breast as if seeking out its shape and texture through the fabric of her shirt. She lifted the shirt, and moaned as he touched her bare skin. His fingertips moved lightly, teasing like feathers, making her squirm with pleasure as they brushed circles around one nipple, then the other.

152

His mouth went away briefly. Then it took a breast, sucking gently, the tongue probing and flicking.

This is how it should be, she thought. Gentle and slow and loving, the desire almost painful, wanting him so badly that nothing else matters. For an instant, she thought of Hoffman cuffed inside the bathroom, only a few yards away, but the image was washed away with a thrilled tremor as Scott's hand slipped under the waistband of her shorts. A finger traced her panties' elastic strip, moving slowly from side to side, lightly scraping her skin, toying with the band.

Lacey pushed a trembling hand down the front of his pants. Sliding it inside his shorts, she felt his hot erection. As she curled her fingers around it, she felt Scott's hand slip into her panties. She gasped as he found her opening. While she stroked his thick shaft, his fingers glided against her, slipped into her, probing and pushing. Her own hand explored Scott, wanting his penis inside her. He eased away. Kneeling beside her, he tugged her pants down. She kicked them off, reached out for him, and opened his trousers. She pulled them down, freed his erection, fondled it, held its burning flesh as he climbed onto her, then guided it between her spread legs.

It sunk into her, filling her, gently pushing deeper and deeper.

'Oh dear God,' she sighed. 'Dear Scott.'

CHAPTER TWENTY-FIVE

DUKANE KNELT alone at the window, staring through its open louvers at the area in front of the house. The low, morning sun made his eyes burn. An effect of going too long without sleep. He closed them. The lids shut out the sunlight, felt soothing on the raw tissue.

He saw Nancy. She winked at him, and lifted her pink nightgown. He expected bare skin, a thatch of pubic hair, perky breasts with upthrust nipples. But no. Not yet. Under the nightgown were red gym shorts and a tank-top. She pulled the top over her head, and there they were, her breasts, firm creamy mounds with nipples erect. She began to dance, whirling, waving the shirt like a flag as her other hand lowered to her gym shorts. But now they were faded blue cut-off jeans. She opened them, continuing to dance, and they slowly slid down her legs. She skipped out of them.

She lay on her back, knees up, thighs apart, rubbing herself with both hands, then beckoning him. But as he approached, he saw jagged shards of glass embedded in her skin. They protruded from her breasts, belly, thighs – glistening, clear blades waiting to rip him up. With a grin, she opened her mouth. Her tongue slid out, weighted with a jagged triangle of glass. Reaching between her legs, she spread her flesh. Powdered glass spilled like salt from her vagina.

'Fuck me,' she said.

'Not till you take the glass out,' he told her.

She spat the chunk from her mouth. It shot out like shrapnel, flipping and twisting toward him. He flinched away. His forehead struck the window sill.

He awoke with a gasp.

'*Christ*,' he muttered, angry at himself for dozing off, and shaken by the dream.

He scanned the area in front of the house. Still no sign of the car or any people. Getting to his feet, he crossed the room. He knelt on the couch and parted the curtains behind it. Fifty feet away stood a garage of white stone. Nobody at its corners or visible on its roof. But off to the left, a hundred yards away, a figure was lying prone on a rise among balls of cacti. Dukane saw a rifle in his arms. He ducked away, and hurried into the kitchen. From its window, he saw another distant sniper.

He filled a glass with water. As he sipped it, he entered the hallway. Scott and Lacey were asleep on the floor, holding each other. He carefully stepped around them, and entered the bedroom. From its window, he spotted another man with a rifle.

At least they're not assaulting the place, he thought. Containing us. Maybe waiting for reinforcements. That would explain why the car hadn't shown up again. One of them must've taken it to alert others.

If the girls got away all right, they'd go for the authorities. An army of cops might descend on the place any time.

Interesting to see which army arrives first.

Setting down his empty glass, he went into the hallway and shook Scott's foot. The man woke with a start. Lacey moaned, but didn't awaken. Scott gently untangled himself from her, and followed Dukane into the living room.

'I want you to take over the watch. They've got snipers stationed on both sides and the rear. Maybe one in front, but I haven't spotted him.'

'All right.'

'I don't think they'll rush us, but we can't rule it out.'

He left Scott by the front window, and went into the kitchen. He searched a utility closet, a cupboard under the sink, and wasn't surprised at not finding what he wanted.

People don't usually store combustibles in the house.

He returned to the living room.

'I'm going out for a second,' he said, unholstering his automatic.

Scott frowned.

'We've gotta get the paint off Hoffman.'

'What for?'

'Have to make him disappear in case the cops show up. That's assuming you're still hot to get his story for yourself.'

'I am. But I don't like the idea of you going outside.'

Dukane slapped his shoulder. 'Buck up, boyo, I'll be back.'

He led Scott to the window over the couch, and pointed out the rifleman. 'I don't expect you to hit him at this range, but put a few rounds close enough to worry him if he starts tracking me.'

With a nod, Scott opened the louvered window.

'You have the keys?'

Scott fished Jan's key case out of his pocket. Dukane took it. He went to the front window.

Scanning the area in front of the house, he saw no one. He pushed open the door and stepped out. Back against the wall, he searched the barren terrain. Odd if nobody was covering the front. If there were only four, though, and one had to drive for help . . . Well, the two at the sides could easily pick off anyone trying to break from the front.

He stepped off the edge of the stoop. Pressing his back to the wall, he made his way toward the corner. Prickles stung his legs, and he looked down to see cactus spines clinging to his trousers. The girls had apparently planted 'jumping cactus' along the wall, a variety that seems to shoot its quills into anyone venturing too close.

Nice of them, he thought.

At the corner, he blinked sweat from his eyes and crouched down. The spines dug into his calves. Ignoring

156

the pain, he peered around the wall's edge. He glimpsed the sniper, saw the rifle aimed his way. Two shots blasted at once. As a bullet whined off the wall inches from his face, he sprang up and dashed for the garage. Gunfire erupted from both the house and sniper, a roar that seemed to jolt the air around him as he ran.

A bullet tugged his sleeve near the shoulder.

Abruptly, there was silence. He threw himself against the side door of the garage, and shoved a key at the lock face.

Didn't fit.

He tried another. This one slid in. He turned it, threw open the door, and burst into the stifling heat of the garage.

There were no windows.

Feeling along the wall, his fingertips found a light switch. He flicked it. A single bulb came on.

No car.

But he smiled as he saw what he wanted.

Lacey, shocked awake by the shooting, grabbed her revolver, scrambled off the makeshift bed, and rushed into the living room. She saw Scott kneeling on the couch, aiming through the open slats of a window.

He glanced around at her.

'Come here,' he said.

She hurried to the window.

'See that guy out there? Dukane's in the garage. He'll be coming out in a minute, and the guy'll try to nail him. Take my place here. I'll go to the front. When Dukane comes out, start shooting.'

'It's too far.'

'Doesn't matter. With fire coming from two angles, he won't know whether to . . .'

'Shit or go blind?'

'Exactly.'

Lacey nodded, and Scott ran out the front door. She cocked the revolver. She lined up the distant man in the sights, glanced away at the garage door, then back to the man. From his location, it looked as if the garage would give Dukane shelter for the first two or three yards. Then he would be in the open.

Her hand was sweaty on the walnut grips.

Too bad the man's so far away, she thought. If he was half that distance, she'd stand a much better chance of hitting him.

Just as well, maybe. She didn't need another killing on her conscience.

The garage door opened. She sighted on the man and held her breath. Then she glanced again at the door. Dukane stepped out, a large metal container in each hand. But he didn't run. Instead, he set them outside the door and vanished into the garage. Moments later, he re-appeared. With a ladder!

He spread the ladder's legs, climbed it, and boosted himself onto the roof of the garage.

He was gone.

Seconds passed. Lacey licked her parched lips.

Then a single gunshot roared in the stillness.

The distant figure of the rifleman lurched as if kicked, and dropped flat.

Dukane climbed down the ladder. He made a thumbs-up gesture toward Lacey, then carried the ladder back into the garage. He picked up the two containers, and strolled across the open area.

He and Scott came into the house, beaming like boys who'd just won a no-hitter.

'Nice play,' Scott said.

'The bastard came too close, first time across. I chick-ened out of the return run.'

'Wonder if we can get his rifle.'

'Not worth the risk. The rear man would pick us off. But I got what I wanted.' He raised the cans: a two-gallon tin of gasoline and a gallon container of turpentine.

Lacey frowned. 'Turpentine? You're going to take the paint off Hoffman?'

'Right.'

'Don't.'

'Could come in very handy. Lacey, you stay out here and keep an eye on the situation. Scott, get your recorder. No time like the present to get his story.'

CHAPTER TWENTY-SIX

Statement of Samuel Hoffman
July 20

OKAY. YOU want me to talk, I'll talk. Give you everything you need to know for your fuckin' book that's gonna get you killed.

I'm Sammy Hoffman. You guys know that, right? Okay. So I'll start with something you don't know. How about this? I banged my English teacher way back in high school. She was a cunt. That's what you do to cunts, bang 'em.

The one I really wanted, it was Lacey. Used to spend all my time looking at her, thinking how she'd look naked, thinking how her tits'd feel, and her ass and her puss. Now I know, now I know. Only wish I'd got her then. She was just sixteen. Should've took her someplace and kept her. But I was chicken shit. She was too damn beautiful. Scared me off. Yeah, well, got her at last. Well worth the wait, I tell you that. You guys oughta have a sample, if you haven't already.

Okay, so I had this hard-on for Lacey but I was scared to touch her and this English teacher bitch pissed me off so I did her instead. Right on top of her desk after school. It was a kick.

I was dumb, then. If I was smart, I'd of turned the bitch's switch off so she couldn't put her mouth on me. But I didn't, and she did.

Adios, Oasis.

So I'm on the road, here and there and everywhere,

160

doing people every chance I get, always on the move. Shit, I've probably got kids from one end of the country to the next, 'less all the hons got themselves scraped. Yeah, well, plenty were probably on the pill.

Left lots of graves, too. Dead men don't yap. Learned my lesson from the English teacher. See, she taught me something, after all. Thought I was stupid.

Stupid, all right. I should've stayed on my own. That was my big mistake.

Klein. Harold Klein. Met him in LA. A bar on La Cienaga. Tiny's Place. We tipped a few, and he saw my piece and we started jabbing and he figures I'm up for some action. Says he needs a driver and he'll pay me a thousand. That sounded good, only he didn't level. Told me he was hitting a Wells Fargo. I park in front of the bank, only he goes in next door to this TV station and blows the face off this anchor gal, Theresa Chung. Remember her?

Okay. We get the fuck out of there and he has me drive up in this canyon and stop. Only instead of pulling out the bucks he owes me, he pulls a Colt automatic. Dead men don't yap, right? Only he didn't figure on Sammy Hoffman, and guess who winds up in the ditch?

Next thing I know, I wake up in the middle of the night with a muzzle up my mouth. Friends of Harold, right? Wrong. Co-workers. They figure, if I'm good enough to put the dark on Harry, I'm good enough for them. Smart fellas.

Too bad I wasn't that smart. I'd of kissed them off.

But I went along, and pretty soon I'm a hot-shot assassin for The Group. They don't want people snooping into their business, you know? Blowing the whistle on them? Snatching off some of their converts for deprogramming? That sort of shit. They set up the hits real good and paid me through the nose and took good care of me. I was living like a fuckin' tycoon.

Who'd I hit? Senator Cramer, for one. Guy was calling for an official investigation. Seems his son got mixed up in

161

the SDF. That's The Group, you know. The Spiritual Development Foundation. Anyway, that's what got me into this piss soup, that bastard from *People* catching a shot of me in the crowd.

Before Cramer was that nigger mayor in Detroit. Jackson? The LA city council explosion, that was me. The New York police commissioner, Barnes. This ain't necessarily in order, you understand. I can give you guys all the details later, when you get me out of this rat trap and take me someplace safe. Give you something to shoot for. If I tell you everything now, you might just let those bastards have me, right? I'm no fool. I'll just whet your appetites a bit, okay?

Remember Dickinson? Heart attack in his office while he was dickin' his secretary? That was me. Tricked up his rubbers. Chavez, the *investigative* reporter? He put his nose into the SDF. The o.d. that put him away, it wasn't self-inflicted: it was Sammy inflicted.

That's just scratching the surface. There's plenty more. Shit, I worked six years for The Group.

Anyhow, it was that *People* shot that put me away. They figure I can't show my face around, so I'm the perfect sucker for their experiment. They're gonna make me invisible, they say. Sure. Invisible. And shit smells like Chanel, right?

Only they do.

Lacey knocked on the door.

'Come on in,' Dukane said.

Lacey opened it, and stepped into the bathroom. The air was pungent with the smell of turpentine. Scott and Dukane, kneeling over Hoffman, were scouring him with washcloths. The small cassette recorder from Scott's attaché case rested on the toilet seat.

Scott smiled up at her. His face was sweaty, damp hair clinging to his forehead. 'How's it going?' he asked.

'One of the men changed positions. He went over to the body. He's still near it.'

162

'They had to correct their field of fire,' Dukane said. Tipping the turpentine can, he dampened his washcloth and started working on Hoffman's shoulder. Most of the back was clear, now. The arms, still painted, remained cuffed behind him. One leg was gone, as if it had been amputated below the rump. Scott was busy cleaning the other.

'How about joining the party?' Hoffman asked. 'I been entertaining these guys with my exploits. Great stuff, I hate you to miss it.'

She ignored him. 'There's plenty of food,' she said. 'Shall I make some breakfast?'

'I'm starving,' Scott said.

'Bacon and eggs all right?'

'Can't eat that shit,' said Hoffman. 'Get me some beef, and don't cook it.'

'What about you, Matt?'

'Bacon and eggs sound fine. I could use some coffee, too.'

'Gonna get me that meat?'

'It's frozen,' she said.

'So unfreeze it.'

She left the bathroom, never mentioning why she had come in. She couldn't ask them to move out, and she certainly had no intention of using the toilet in front of them. In a kitchen cupboard, she found a plastic pitcher. She lowered her pants and squatted over it. When she finished, she flung its contents out the front door. Then she washed her hands, and set about preparing breakfast.

Guess she didn't want to hear, huh? I get the feeling she don't like me.

Anyway, The Group's got this lab. It's out in Iowa, looks just like a farm. Even grow stuff there. The lab's underground, all kinds of security. Make up all their shit there: potions, amulets, stuff like that. Witchin' shit.

Okay, they take me to the lab. I figure I'm in for it. I mean, how they gonna make a guy invisible, you know? I figure I'm in for shots, at least. God only knows. You don't make a guy invisible with food coloring.

But they don't put me in a cell or a dissection room or nothing, they put me up in a nice room above ground. I've even got my own little enclosed garden right outside my door. This isn't so bad after all, I figure.

And it gets even better. These two gals come in, and they're both fantastic knock-outs. One of them, the gal in charge of the project, she's . . . you'd have to see her. Give you wet dreams. But man, I know right off I'd be in deep shit if I crossed her. It's her eyes. She has this look like she wouldn't mind eating your heart. Well, that wasn't what I wanted eaten so I figured I'd keep off her.

The other, her assistant, wasn't any slouch but she didn't have that wicked look so I was hoping to get a piece of her.

Okay, they're in charge. They're witches, and the gorgeous one turns out to be the leader of the whole ball of wax. Laveda herself. I'd worked six years for her, never seen her. Keeps herself a low profile.

They come in one morning before dawn, it's a Wednesday, with a sack. Laveda tells me to open it. I do, and inside is this guy's head. Nothing else, just his head. A fresh one.

'What am I supposed to do?' I say. 'Eat it?' They don't even crack smiles. Instead, Laveda hands me these black beans and tells me what to do.

I'm not a squeamish guy, you know? I was okay, sticking the beans in his mouth and ears and nose. Then it came to the eyes. You oughta try it sometime. I've gouged a few eyes in my time, but I never stuck around to inspect the damage. Anyway, okay, I popped this guy's eyes and stuck the beans in and shut the lids. Made my skin crawl.

Then they give me a shovel and we go out in my little garden and I have to dig a hole. It only has to be a foot deep. When I'm done, we all get naked. I figure, this is getting better and better. Maybe next is an orgy, who knows? I'd heard plenty about Laveda and her orgies.

Okay, the three of us are standing there bare-ass in the dark, with Coral hanging onto the head. Laveda's wearing this gold chain belt with a dagger at one side and a gold flask on the other. She takes out the dagger. Coral gets on her knees and holds out the head.

What Laveda does then, she starts carving a design on the guy's forehead. Looks like a figure-eight with x's in the middle.

Okay. After she's done with the cutting, she takes the flask off her belt and opens it and holds it up at the sky. 'The river flows,' she says. 'Its water is the water of life. All powerful is he who drinks at its shore.' She takes two drinks out of the flask, and some of it runs off her chin and I see it ain't Scotch, it's blood. Then she takes a mouthful of the stuff and gets the guy's head from Coral and spits it right into his mouth.

Coral does the same thing. Two gulps for her, one for the goddamn head. Then it's my turn. I've done a lot of shit, but I'm no fuckin' vampire. You oughta try a swig of blood, sometime. Put you off your appetite for a week. But that wasn't the worst, the worst was putting my mouth up to this guy's mouth. I didn't want to shut my eyes, you know, and have the gals think I couldn't take it. So I stare the poor dead bastard right in the face and hold his mouth open and try to spit in the blood without touching his lips. But I touched them, all right. And his mouth couldn't hold all this blood, you know, so it came slopping back like he was puking.

Shit. Enough of that. So much for my goddamn orgy. We plant the head face-up, and that's it. The gals slip into their clothes again. *Adios*, see you tomorrow.

I brushed my teeth so hard my gums bled and I figured it was more of *his* blood, and the harder I brushed the more blood came out. I figured the only way to get all the blood out was to upchuck. Didn't do that. It might break the spell, or whatever, and we'd have to go through the whole thing again. So I finally quit brushing, and gargled a lot with Irish, and spent the rest of the day killing the bottle.

The next morning, Coral comes in alone. She's got a bottle under one arm, and I'm hoping it isn't blood. It's Remy Martin. Not for me, though. It's for our pal in the garden. She has me water the fuckin' head with it. A whole fifth of cognac. I suggest we save some for ourselves – I mean, is *he* gonna miss a couple of shots? But she doesn't go for it. Doesn't go for me, either, when I try out a few moves on her.

Okay, we keep this up for a week. Every morning, she wakes me up and we go out with a fresh bottle to dump on the ground.

I keep putting moves on her, and she's getting more bitchy all the time. But I figure I'll get her, sooner or later. One way or the other.

The eighth day, Laveda's with her. She tells me to keep my hands off Coral, and I figure it out. They're a couple of dykes, right? Says she'll cut off my cock . . . Yeah, well, she hasn't yet. The cunt.

Anyway, after she lays this on me we go out to the garden and get naked, and Laveda starts this chanting shit, holding up a fifth of Remy. I was cold sober. I never do drugs. Maybe she had me hypnotized or something, who knows? But anyway, pretty soon I hear this other voice – a man's voice. Coming out of nowhere. It says, 'What are you doing?'

Laveda hands me the bottle. 'Say, "I'm watering my head." '

So I say it.

'Let me water the head,' the voice says.

'Tell him "no." '

So I tell him no.

Then the dirt over the head starts to move, like a finger's drawing in it. It draws the same design, that figure-eight with the x's, like Laveda cut in the guy's forehead.

'Now he may water your head,' Laveda tells me.

'Go ahead,' I say.

166

Something snatches the bottle out of my hand and it falls to the ground and the cognac spills out. That's it. We get dressed, and the gals take off.

I spent a while out there looking for a speaker. Figured there might be one hidden around somewhere. But if there was, I didn't find it.

The next morning, Laveda and Coral come back. First we strip down, then I have to dig up the head. What a fuckin' sight it was. They made me take out the beans, dig 'em right out of his ears and nostrils and mouth and . . . and out of his eye holes. The beans'd sprouted a little, by then. Laveda held up this mirror and told me to put one of the beans in my mouth. 'Don't swallow it,' she told me. She didn't have to tell me that.

I put one in my mouth, like she said, and held it in my cheek like a wad of chewing tobacco. Only it didn't taste like tobacco. It tasted like a rotten fuckin' corpse.

Anyway, I look at the mirror and *bango*, I'm gone.

Lacey knocked on the bathroom door and entered. 'Breakfast is . . .'

On the floor where Hoffman had been, she saw six bandages: three hovering several inches above the tile, the others pressed against it. And she saw his silver penis and scrotum. He lay on his back, one handcuff around a leg of the sink.

'Just in time,' Hoffman said.

Dukane poured turpentine onto a washcloth. The cloth left his hand, moved through the air, and began to stroke the penis.

'He's *free*?'

'Just one hand,' Scott told her.

'All I need,' said Hoffman, rubbing himself to an erection. 'Squeamish guys. Don't want to touch my dick. How about you?' He flung the cloth at Lacey. It slapped her upraised arm, and she knocked it away. 'Rather lick me? Wouldn't get the paint off, but it'd get *me* off.'

'Shut up!' Scott yelled.

'Touchy touchy. This guy's got a hard-on for you, hon. Don't we all?'

Dukane pounded down, his fist hammering the emptiness near the bandages.

Hoffman grunted.

Lacey hurried from the bathroom. 'Breakfast is on the table,' she called back.

She rushed into the kitchen, breathing deeply, fighting her revulsion. Afraid she might vomit, she bent over the kitchen sink.

'That guy's an animal,' Scott said, stepping up behind her.

'Stop maligning animals.'

He laughed softly, and kissed her bare shoulder.

CHAPTER TWENTY-SEVEN

OKAY, WHERE was I? Oh yeah, just popped a bean in my mouth. Just like that, I'm gone. I look down and can't see nothing – no legs, no dick, no nothing. I feel myself. I'm all there, just like normal, only I can't see myself. I give Coral's tits a squeeze and watch 'em bunch up, and Laveda stabs me in the back with a fuckin' dagger.

Hurts like shit. I go down, wondering why they went to all the trouble making me invisible if they're gonna kill me.

Laveda says, 'I warned you not to touch her.' Then she tells me I'll be okay, I can't be killed 'less I'm hit in a vital place like my heart or a big artery or I'm burnt, or something; I've drunk at the river and I'm all powerful and I'll heal up in no time flat. She tells me to get up, and I do. I can feel myself bleeding for a while, but pretty soon it stops.

She tells me to take the bean out of my mouth. I do, and *presto* I'm there again.

Long as I've got one of the beans in my mouth, she says, I'll be invisible. When I spit it out, you can see me again. But if I swallow one, it's so long Sammy for weeks, maybe months. It'll digest, see, and some of it'll get in my system. Long as any's in my system, I stay invisible.

Then Laveda lets me know what it's all about. She's got big plans for me. Tomorrow, I'm supposed to head off for DC and do a job on the President, the VP, the Speaker of the House. Presto, instant chaos. That's just the thing for Laveda and her bunch. They'll be free to do whatever they want. And it'll be a cinch for me, right? I can go anywhere, do anything. I can't be stopped. I pretend it's a great idea.

Well that night, I get a few ideas of my own. Laveda's right, I can go anywhere and do whatever I please; I could think of plenty of stuff I'd rather do than spend the rest of my life knocking off people for The Group.

So I strip and pop a bean in my mouth, and do a little exploring. I explore my way right into Laveda's room, which turns out to be just down the hall. Coral's there, too. Just like I figured.

They're sitting around gabbing. Turns out, I'm the first guy they've done this number on. Laveda'd tried it herself, a year ago, and Coral's saying how she'd like a crack at being invisible.

Laveda sort of puts her off. I think I know why, too. Reason she hasn't gone around making lots of her people invisible. It gives them too much power. She wants all the power for herself, wants to stay in control. She just made me invisible to get a job done for her. And I figure I'm probably expendable, she'll wipe me out once I get it done.

Well, they finally leave off their jabber and get down to rolling on the bed. You should've seen those two go at each other. Grunting and groaning, licking, eating each other out. I almost popped my load, just watching. Must've gone on for an hour. I wanted to jump right on 'em and stick it in the nearest hole, but I held off. Didn't want to mess with Laveda. The gal's bad news.

They finally get done. I see Coral making for the john, so I get in quick ahead of her. She starts taking a shower. Okay, I know Laveda's out in the other room and if she gets me, I've had it. But I'm invisible, right? How's she gonna hurt me if she can't find me?

So I climb into the shower with Coral. She suspects something when the door slides open, but before she has a chance to yell I bash her head on the tile and knock her out. More than out, dead. So then I lay her down in the tub and have my fun. You ever let it go after holding back for an hour? Nothing like it. Thought I'd bust, I came so hard.

Okay, I get out of the tub and dry off – don't want to be tracking water, you know. Then I get scared 'cause I see myself in the fuckin' mirror! It isn't me, really. The place is all steamy and there I am, like a hole in it. Bad news! I wanted to get outa there. So I hurried and finished drying, and snuck open the door a crack, just enough to see out. Laveda was on the bed. Looked like she was asleep.

I spent a lot of time watching her, wondering if I oughta turn off her switch. I mean, I knew I should. The bitch and her whole bunch would be after me for doing her playmate, and I'd be up shit creek if they ever got their hands on me. But I tell you what, I was scared. You'd be scared too. She's not what you'd call normal. I figured, what if I made a try for her and I couldn't kill her no matter what I did? She's got this magic, right? I finally figure I'm not gonna chance it. I'll just pull a vanishing act.

So I sneak out and get back to my room for the rest of the beans. Then it's *adios*.

No sweat at all, getting out of the compound. I walked right past the guards. Nothing there for them to see, except the beans in my hand, and those aren't big enough that anybody'd notice. The one in my mouth, that's invisible. Guess 'cause it's mixed up in my spit. I figured out, after a bit, I could pop 'em all in my mouth when I needed to hide 'em. Smart, huh? Better than leaving the things behind when I wanted to sneak in someplace: lost two, that way.

Okay, so I'm out of the compound and walking down this road. It's three miles, all of it through Group property, till I get to a highway. Remember now, I'm not only bare-ass, I'm bare*foot*. You try walking three miles barefoot, sometime.

I wanted a car bad. You get out in the sticks around midnight and see how many cars go by. Zip. And the ones that did come along, how was I gonna stop 'em? I finally made it to a farmhouse, dog tired. Speaking of dogs, that's where I ran into my first. I don't know if they can see me or what, but they sure as shit know where to find me. This one at the farm raised hell, even took a nip out of my leg before I killed it.

Farmer Joe came out to snoop around, and that gave me a chance to get inside. I waited till he was back in bed, then got a knife and went upstairs and slit his gullet. Got the wife, too. They had three kids. Just one was a girl. I had a good time with her.

After that, I wanted to sack out. But what am I gonna do with the bean in my mouth? Don't want it falling out while I'm asleep. So I just went ahead and swallowed it.

I woke up, after a couple of hours, when this car pulled up in front. There's Laveda, and half a dozen guys from the compound. The guys are wearing these weird masks. What they are, I figure out later, they're infra-red gadgets. Put on one of those suckers, and you can see me. See my heat image. Those bastards from The Group think of everything.

Okay, I figured they wouldn't know for sure I was there. They might think I just did my business and moved on, long as they didn't see me. So I hid. I ran over to the boys' room, and dumped the crap out of their toy box and hid in there. Sure enough, they didn't find me. Spent half an hour turning the house, then gave up.

But the fuckers set the place on fire. Insurance, I guess. Just in case they'd missed me. Tells you something, don't it? Sure told *me* something. Told me they wanted my ass dead.

I just about cooked, but I got out of that place. Their car was gone. Great, I'm home free. Then I catch a slug in the shoulder and go down. This is it, Sammy. They'll move in now, and Laveda'll get your dick just like she said. Except *they* don't move in. Just this one guy comes out from beside the garage, decked out with a rifle and

172

those infra-red goggles. I play dead, and he's dumb enough to come close and it's bye-bye dummy. I grab the rifle out of his hands and ram it through his teeth and blast off the back of his head.

Then I go over to the garage and hot-wire one of Farmer Joe's cars, and get the fuck out of there.

Lacey threw open the bathroom door. 'A car's coming!'

'Cops?' Dukane asked.

'I don't think so.'

She ran ahead of them, pressing her shirt to her damp breasts.

After cleaning the breakfast dishes, she had given in to her need to clean herself. She filled the sink with warm water, then checked the windows to be certain the snipers remained in their normal positions. Returning to the kitchen, she used liquid detergent to wash her hair. Bent over the sink to rinse, she worried about leaving the house unguarded, imagined the front door bursting open, men with guns rushing in. As soon as the soap was out of her hair, she grabbed a hand towel and again checked the windows.

Everything looked all right.

But she didn't like the kitchen, felt blind at its sink, and vulnerable. So she filled two pans with water and carried them into the living room. Facing the front window, she took off her clothes. She sponged herself with warm soapy water, and wiped the slickness away with cool water from the other pan. It felt very good. Maybe later, once the men were done in the bathroom, she would ask them to move Hoffman out and she could take a real bath. When was the last time? Yesterday? Just before going out to dinner with Scott. Only yesterday. It seemed like weeks ago.

She squeezed the sponge against the nape of her neck and felt the cool water stream down her back. It slid over her buttocks and between them, and trickled down the backs of her legs. If Scott were here, he could wash her back . . .

She imagined him coming into the room, and smiling with delight when he saw her. She would turn to face him. He would kiss her mouth, her neck, her breasts. His tongue would prod her nipples.

Rather lick me?

The memory of Hoffman's words smashed her fantasy. She tossed the sponge into the water and picked up a dish towel. She patted her legs dry. She rubbed between them. She looked around at the cut on her buttock. It was slightly red at the edges, but scabbed over. It hadn't been much more than a scratch, after all. But it itched more than the others that threaded her body. She resisted an urge to rake it with her fingernails, but rubbed it gently with the towel.

As she started to dry her arms, the sound of a car engine froze her. She glanced out the window. A black Rolls Royce sped up the road toward the house.

Whipping the towel around her waist, she scooped up her shirt and raced for the bathroom.

Now Scott and Dukane were rushing past her, pistols ready. Scott checked the side window. Dukane kicked over a water pan as he dashed to the front. He crouched at the window.

Scott ran to the hall.

Lacey pulled her shirt on, grabbed her revolver off the rocking chair, and knelt beside Dukane. The car had stopped in front of the door – no more than ten yards away. Through its tinted windows, she saw moving, indistinct shapes.

A door flew open. A naked woman was thrust from the car. She fell facedown, and the door slammed shut.

Her back and rump were striped with raw, bleeding wounds. She pushed herself up. On her knees, she looked at the window. Lacey moaned, cold with sickness as she recognized the swollen, bloody face. Jan. The flesh of her chest and belly was tattered. Blood spilled from open wounds where her nipples should have been, flowed from her vagina, sheathing her thighs, forming a puddle on the ground between her knees.

The rear window slid down three inches. Lacey saw the crown of a bald head inside the car.

'We want Hoffman,' a man's voice called through the opening. 'Give us Hoffman, and we'll let the rest of you go. If you're . . .'

Dukane fired. With the first shot, the pale scalp erupted and dropped from sight. The second shot smashed into the window, halfway down, blasting out a cone of glass but not breaking through.

The car sprang forward.

Until that instant, Lacey didn't see the cord – the white electrical cord around Jan's left ankle and running up to the crack at the bottom of the car door. It snapped taut. Tugged Jan's leg from under her. Dragged her, spinning and bouncing, alongside the car.

Lacey's own scream drowned out the screams from Jan. Covering her ears, she lowered her head and shut her eyes tight.

Finally, she raised her head. The car had turned around and was now speeding back. Its body hid Jan from her view until it turned right and headed up the entry drive. Then she glimpsed the tumbling carcass.

Throwing herself away from the window, she grabbed the nearer pan and vomited into it. As convulsions wracked her, she realized vaguely that her towel had fallen away. It didn't matter. Her mind reeled at what she'd seen. Would they do the same to Nancy? To her? Lacey's stomach was empty, now, but she strained with dry heaves. Her mouth dripped hot stomach fluids. Her eyes dripped tears.

'You stay with Lacey,' Scott told Dukane. 'I'd better go in and get the rest of Hoffman's story.'

Dukane helped Lacey to the couch. Lying on it, she felt the soft fabric against her buttocks. She pulled a pillow down to cover her bare groin.

'What about Nancy?' she asked.

'There's nothing we can do.'

Dukane handed the panties and shorts to Lacey. 'We could give them Hoffman,' she said.

He turned away, and sat on an edge of the coffee table. As Lacey put on her clothes, he said. 'They won't let us go.'

'Why not?'

'Several reasons. First, we killed some of their people: the cops in Tucson, the sniper, the guy in the car just now. They can't let us get away with that. Second, we've been in contact with Hoffman and they've got to assume he talked, maybe gave out the formula for becoming invisible.'

'Did he?'

'He did. That, plus plenty of other information. The Group can't allow that. How many reasons is that?'

'Two.'

'Three, even if the other reasons didn't exist, they'd want us for the sport. The people in The Group are evil. I've had some prior experience with them. I know. They love the power, love to make people cringe at their feet, to torture and kill for their own pleasure.'

'Doesn't sound good,' Lacey said.

'It's not.'

CHAPTER TWENTY-EIGHT

OKAY, I'M tooling along in Farmer Joe's car, keeping a sharp look-out for the bunch from the compound. But I never do see 'em. The farmhouse was north of the compound, so they must've figured I'd keep going that way. Well, I didn't. I went east. Got clean away.

But it gets to be daylight, and there's some traffic on the highway, and I start getting queer looks from the jerks in the other cars. Doesn't take me long to figure out why. I'm invisible, right? So who's driving my car?

I don't give much shit where I'm going – long as it's not back to the compound – so I pull into a Denny's and climb in back of the first car I find unlocked. Wherever they're going, I'll go. So I'm sitting there in the backseat and along comes not just momma and poppa, but three brats. Being invisible's no cinch. When the door opens, I knock this little bastard on his ass and get out of there. The kid's bawling, tells his dad somebody *pushed* him, and the old man gives him a whack for fibbing. Nice guy.

Next time, I play it safe. A guy comes in the parking lot alone. I make sure he doesn't lock up, then I go in Denny's, in the kitchen there, and heist myself a coke and a couple of burgers and polish 'em off while I wait for the guy.

He takes me into Iowa City, to this university there. I find my way into a girls' dorm. I tell you, thought I'd died and gone to heaven. Plenty of food for the taking, found me an empty room, and *man* the girls! You should've seen those hons in the showers.

There's one in particular, comes in for a shower every night around nine. A real honey, looks like a movie star, tits out to here. I'm sitting down so the steam won't give me away. Front row seat. Watching her rub herself all over with soap. I've got a hard-on feels like it's gonna bust.

Well, this one night I can see she's hot. Not just washing, you know, but feeling herself, rubbing her tits, playing around with her puss. Finally, she gets on her back with her legs up so the water's hitting her quiff. I move in with my mouth. I'm licking and sucking and sticking my tongue in, and she's so far gone she doesn't know, like she thinks the spray's doing it. Maybe she thought she was dreaming, I don't know. Well, she's squirming and moaning and rubbing her tits, and I just go ahead and put my dick right in. Should've seen her eyes bug out. Looks down at herself. Reaches down. I pull it out and give her a handful. She feels it up and down, like trying to figure out if it's what she thinks. She looks real confused and scared, at first. Then she gets this funny little smile on her face, and puts it back in.

I go ahead and hump the daylights out of her. She damn near screams when she comes.

After we're done, she starts drying herself off, frowning like she's trying to figure something out. Then she says, 'Are you here?'

I take the towel, and finish drying her.

'What are you?' she asks.

I don't answer.

'Am I . . . imagining you? I've never . . . here I am, talking to myself. Shit.' Then she reaches out and touches me, touches my dick. 'You sure don't *feel* like an hallucination.' She gets this funny smile again, and goes down on her knees and sucks me off. 'Don't taste like one, either,' she says when she's finished. 'Whatever you are, I hope you don't go away.'

'I'm the invisible man,' I whisper.

'No shit?'

'A government experiment went haywire. They're after me. 'Fraid I'll spill the beans.' A good one, right? Spill the beans? Anyway, I tell her I'm hiding out 'cause they'll kill me, which wasn't that far from the truth. If The Group ever got their hands on me . . .

Well, this gal's fascinated. Says I can hide out in her room, and she'll take care of me.

And she does. Man, does she take care of me! A real wild gal. Name was Robin, like the bird. The first couple days, she cut all her classes and stayed in the room with me. Only just left to get us food. Told all her friends she'd come down with something. It was like a fuckin' honeymoon. Didn't do nothing but play games.

That, and talk. A great talker, Robin. Name me a woman that isn't. She wanted to know the story of my life. I just made up a lot of shit, made me sound like a regular sweetheart. Most of all, she wanted to know how I got invisible, and what it was like. Said she wished she was that way, she'd do just what I did except she'd head over to the boys' shower room. I let her know it wasn't all fun and games, like how you freeze your ass off when it's cold out, and how tough it is to get places. Like how do you drive?

So she drags out her make-up and shows me how to put it on so I've got a face. Puts a wig on me. Presto, I've got a head. After a couple of days, I have her go out and buy me some clothes and sunglasses. Now I'm all set. I don't look like much. Look kind of weird, in fact, and even weirder when my mouth's open, but I figure at least I'll be able to get around at night like a human being.

Robin's got other ideas, too. She's full of ideas. It's June, see, and she's got final exams coming up. So she puts me to work hiding out in faculty offices and heisting exams. Stupid stuff, but it gave me something to do and kept her happy.

She also wants to even up a score. Her boyfriend dumped her for some bitch. They're living off campus, so she drives me out there to take care of them. She just wants me to do some tricks, move some furniture around, make stuff float, scare the shit out of 'em. But the gal turns out to be a fox so after I spook 'em for a while, I do the guy, tear him up, chase the gal around with his head, have my own kind of fun.

Well, Robin finds out all about it when she sees the newspaper. Calls me a maniac, shit like that. Frankly, I think she's just pissed 'cause I fucked the gal. But she's also yelling about how the cops'll come looking for her, seeing as she was the jilted lover. I figure she's probably right. The cops'll pull her in and she'll finger me. So it's *adios* Robin. I break her neck and light out.

I take along her make-up, and the clothes she bought me, and my six beans. I hide in a utility closet till night, then get the hell out of the dorm and steal her car. She isn't gonna need it, right?

The car's hot, though. I'm no dummy. I know I've gotta dump it fast. So I drive downtown – what there is of it – and I see where a movie's just getting out. None of the gals coming out of the theater are alone, so I follow this guy. When he gets to his car, I bash him. I scoot him over to the passenger seat, and bring my stuff over to his car.

Smart, huh? Look at it this way: if I heist a car, somebody's gonna miss it and call the cops. Probably by morning. There I am, stuck with another hot car before I hardly get used to it. But if I take the guy with it, he's not gonna tell his car's gone, right? Dead men don't yap. And if a guy goes to the movies alone, you can lay odds he's single. Won't be a wife waiting up for him, worrying her tail off. So I figure I can use the car for a couple of days, at least, maybe longer. You ever need a car for a long haul, kill off the driver.

Anyway, once I've got the guy's car, I drive out in the boondocks, throw him in the trunk, and put on my make-up and clothes so I'll pass for a normal person.

I'm on the road a long time, after that. I drive at night. Rip off restaurants and houses for food. Sleep in the backseat when daylight hits, either that or take a house. I found one place where the folks were on vacation or something. Stayed there a week. But most of the time, the places weren't deserted and I had to do the people.

Couldn't stay more than a day or two, then, 'cause sure enough somebody'd come around snooping.

Then it'd get in the papers. Goddamn papers. I know The Group, see, know they're watching out for stuff like that. Probably sticking pins in a map. Not gonna quit till they've got my ass nailed.

So then I get this bright idea. I grab a camper, an RV, off a couple of old farts I figure are retired and nobody's gonna miss 'em for a while. Then I head west. Keep my hands to myself, don't leave a trail for the fuckin' Group.

First thing you know, I'm in Phoenix. I figure, hey, how about paying a visit to my old friends in Oasis?

CHAPTER TWENTY-NINE

'GIVE US Hoffman!'

The voice startled Lacey awake. She raised her head off the couch and saw Dukane crouched by the front window.

'Give us Hoffman,' the tinny voice continued, 'and we'll let you live.'

Lacey rushed to Dukane's side. Looking out the window, she saw the black Rolls Royce stopped in front of the house – perhaps thirty feet away. The doors on its far side stood open, but the body of the car hid whatever was being done.

'I warn you,' said the amplified voice. Lacey spotted its source: a man on a distant rise of land, speaking into a megaphone. 'Give us Hoffman, or you will all be annihilated. There is no escape for you unless you do as we ask. You have seen what we do to our enemies. Each of you will meet a similar end, if you continue to ignore our request.' The megaphone was lowered.

Lacey heard the bathroom door open. Scott rushed across the floor and knelt at the other window.

From behind the car came a heavy clank. A hammer striking metal? The pounding continued with a slow, even rhythm.

'What're they doing?'

Scott frowned at Lacey, and she saw anguish in his eyes. He backhanded speckles of sweat off his upper lip. 'Maybe you shouldn't watch.'

'You think it's Nancy?'

'Yeah.'

Dukane suddenly rushed from the room.

The pounding stopped for a few seconds, then started

again. Lacey scurried over to Scott's window.

'Sounds like they're driving in stakes,' he said.

'Oh God.' Lacey sank down. Turning, she sat beneath the window with her back against the wall. She brought up her legs, hugged them to her breasts, pressed her mouth to one knee.

The slow pounding kept on.

Dukane returned to the room, crouching low, a wine bottle in hand.

'Nobody's moving in,' he said, and squatted near the other front window. 'Can you tell what they're doing?'

'Driving in stakes, I think.'

'Shit,' he muttered. He took a handkerchief from his pocket, tore it in half, and twisted one of the pieces into a strip. He stuffed it into the bottle's mouth, and drew it out. The pungent fumes of gasoline stung Lacey's nostrils.

He reversed the rag and stuffed it into the bottle again. Three inches hung out like a wick.

The pounding outside continued.

'Anybody got a match?'

Lacey hurled herself forward, scurried to the coffee table, and grabbed a lighter. She raced back to Dukane.

'When I open the door, light the rag.'

Lacey nodded, suddenly excited, eager to be striking back.

Dukane jerked the door open.

Lacey lighted the wick. As fire bloomed from the dripping rag, Dukane pitched the bottle. He slammed the door shut and dived into Lacey, throwing her to the floor as bullets burst through the wood above them. Splinters rained down.

Dukane rolled off, and scrambled to his window. Lacey saw Scott take aim. She rushed to his side as the flaming car lunged forward, its far doors still open, leaving two men behind. One raced after it, yelling, his open Hawaiian shirt fluttering behind him like a cape. He turned a somersault as Scott's bullet smacked the back of his head. The other man, on his knees with a hammer when the car left

183

him unprotected, sprang to his feet. He ran toward the house, waving the hammer overhead like the tomahawk of a demented Apache.

'Let him come!' Dukane yelled. 'We can use him.'

His naked body, as bony as a starved man, was streaked with blood. Not his own, Lacey assumed. What had he been doing? She was afraid to look away from him. He ran toward the window, shrieking, and looked about to dive through when a dozen bullets hit him from behind.

Scott threw Lacey back.

The man's head drove into the window as if trying to squeeze itself between two of the flat, open slats of glass. They burst, tearing his scalp, ripping the sides of his face and neck. His chin came to rest on the sill. Blood slid down the inside of the wall.

Lacey scooted backwards, unable to look away from the ghastly man's head. 'Get . . . get him *out* of here!' she stammered. 'Get him OUT!'

'Oh good Christ,' Dukane said. He was staring out his window. 'My God, those . . .!' Leaping away from the window, he took quick strides toward the dead man's protruding head.

'What did they . . .?'

'*Bastards!*' Dukane swung up his leg in a vicious kick, catching the man in the face. The head bounded upward. Lacey glimpsed its torn, mashed face. The eyes seemed to glare at her with hatred for an instant as the head smashed through three more louvers. Then it dropped backwards out of sight.

Scott ran to the window. He knelt beside it and looked out. 'Oh no,' he muttered. He turned to Dukane, his face ashen. 'What'll we do?'

'Nothing.'

'*Nothing?*'

'We can't get to her. They'd nail us before we got a yard.'

'We can't just leave her like that!'

'Want to put her out of misery?'

'No! My God, Matt! I don't think she's even hurt.'

'Hard to tell.'

'I think she's all right. But my God, we can't just . . . Stop!' he told Lacey, raising his hand like a traffic cop as she crawled forward. 'You don't want to see it.'

'What? What did they do to her? You said she's all right.'

'They've got her staked down. With Jan.'

'Jan?'

'What's left of her,' Dukane muttered. 'They're tied face to face.'

CHAPTER THIRTY

I'M IN the camper, right? I'm not gonna take it to Oasis, though. Suppose somebody digs up the old farts? I don't want their RV popping up where I'm at. So I ditch it at the Phoenix airport, along with my clothes and make-up, and don't take nothing with me but my four beans. I'd lost two, by then. But the one I'd eaten was still doing its job. Still is. That's close to two months, right?

Okay, I take a Greyhound to Oasis. Leave the driving to them. The thing was nearly empty, so I didn't have no trouble.

First thing I do when I get there, I look up my old pal Lacey in the phone book. Only her name ain't in it. I figure she's either unlisted, or she's got herself married, or she's moved on. I can't exactly stop someone on the street and ask, right? If she's in Oasis, though, I'm gonna find her.

So what I do, I head for the old lady's market. Too much going on in the Safeway, people gonna be tripping over me. The market's quiet, I know my way around. Hell, I damn near lived in that dump when I was a kid. After school, weekends. Beat the shit out of me if I gave 'em any lip about it.

Well, this is my chance to pay the old lady back. Spook her up, and do her. But first I'm gonna lay low. If Lacey's still in town, she's gonna pop up in the market sooner or later. Everybody does. Even the Safeway regulars, they show up for a frozen pizza or aspirin or some kind of odds and ends. So I'll just hang out and wait.

Only trouble is, the old bat's got ears like a hawk. I don't even make it through the first day, and she hears me

186

moving around. It's night, about an hour before closing time, when suddenly she perks up and starts acting scared and looking all over for me.

Well, I like seeing her scared. Gives me a kick, throwing a fright into folks, but she's special. I'm thinking of all the times she used to slam me around, whip me with the ironing cord. Her and the old man both. Too bad *he* kicked off before I got a chance at him, the old turd. Anyway, she's plenty scared 'cause of the noises, so I throw another one into her by opening up the cash register. That does it. She closes and high-tails it.

I'm pissed, right? There goes my big plan for laying low and waiting for Lacey to show up. So I'm eating a steak and soaking up a bottle of red to make myself feel better when some asshole starts pounding on the door. I toss a fuckin' meat cleaver at him. Too bad I missed.

So what happens next? A whole troop comes piling into the store. The old lady, the jerk that was at the door, some other gal, and guess who? My old pal, Lacey. Things are looking up, right? Only they take one look at the cleaver stuck in the door, and run off like the joint's haunted.

I go after 'em. By the time I get to the door, though, they're packed in this car and taking off.

Well, at least I know Lacey's still in town.

A cop shows up, a little later. I just stand around and watch him search. When he takes off, I sack out in the storeroom.

That was Friday night. I figured the old cow'd be back in the morning, but she didn't open up all weekend. Spooked her good, I guess. Anyway, she comes in Monday morning and sees the mess I'd made. She always did hate messes. She wasn't so scared, this time. Just pissed off. People came in, she'd tell 'em it was vandals, probably kids. If they come back, she says, she's gonna fix their wagon.

So that night, some pal of hers shows up with a fuckin' watchdog. I get out of there till they leave, 'cause the dog's gonna go for me, you know. Well, once they're gone I sneak in again to take care of the mutt. It damn near got me, but I opened up its head with the meat cleaver and ripped the thing apart. Then I skinned it. Even tried some. I figure, shit, it tried to take a bite out of me. Turn-about's fair play. Didn't taste bad.

I figure all hell's gonna break loose when they find what's left of the dog, so I get out of there before morning.

Head over to the high school. Forgot school's out for the summer, till I got there. But it turns out they've got summer school going, and most of it's athletic stuff. So I'm okay, after all.

Guess where I go? Where else, the girls' shower room. I've got a thing about shower rooms, huh? When I was a kid, I used to always dream about getting into this one, grabbing a peek at all those hons, maybe copping a feel here and there. Used to wish I could turn invisible, and just spend all day with 'em. Well, I knew that was impossible. Impossible, right? So I thought I'd dress up like a girl and sneak in that way. Figured I'd get caught, though. Well, now I'm invisible and I make my dream come true.

These hons are a lot younger than the ones at the university. Some are still flat, some got these tiny little pointed tits that look like they're half nipple, and some got boobs out to here. Some haven't even got a bush, yet.

I have a great time watching, sometimes grabbing a little feel. Tell you how you do it. I worked out a system at the university. You go for where their hands are. They're rubbing soap on their pussy, you can get in a feel without them noticing. See what I mean?

Anyway, around noon, things slow down in the shower department. Only a few in there, rinsing off after their volleyball and stuff. One's this blonde with nifty little pointed tits. I follow her home. The house is empty, which works out nicely. I don't want her knowing my secret, so I bop her on the head. Then I blindfold and gag her. Wait till she comes around before I start the fun and games.

You'll be happy to know I didn't kill her. No point. Just draw attention to myself, right? The way I did it, she maybe kept it to herself. You live in a little town like Oasis, you don't want it getting around you've been raped. People figure you brought it on yourself, you'll never live it down. So I just left her, and headed on back to the market.

Guess who's there. Not just my old lady, but the asshole that owned the dog. He's got himself a shotgun. And he doesn't go away. He's gonna blow the head off the bastard that put the dark on his pooch. So he says.

The store's full of people. They're all buying one or two things, just for an excuse to visit the scene of the crime. Must be eight o'clock before the joint clears out.

That's when I go to it. Start spooking 'em. The asshole almost gets me with his shotgun, though. Blows apart a coke display. Then I take his shotgun away and knock him on the head. I don't have time to finish the job, 'cause the old lady's screaming her face off and running for the door.

I catch up to her, throw her down, and tell her who I am. It's Sammy, her darling son, come back to give her a taste of what she'd given him.

She's crying and pleading with me, saying she's sorry. Man, is she sorry. Especially when I start snapping her fingers. I have to gag her to stop the screams. Then I drag her back to the meat counter.

She and the old turd taught me how to be a butcher, how to use the bone saw and cleaver. Made me sick. All that blood. But then I got to like it, and they'd catch me eating the raw meat and they'd say I was stealing and knock me around. Well, they got their way. Made me into a butcher.

So here goes the old bag, up on the chopping block. I go at her real slow, wanting to keep her alive for a while so she can see what a good butcher she turned out. I even use tourniquets on her stumps to keep the bleeding down so she'll last a while longer.

Hope she enjoyed it.

Packaged her up real nice in cellophane, and laid her out with the rest of the beef. Then I went over to the guy.

He's still out cold. I start with his arm. Hack it right off. And then I hear the front door open.

If it ain't my old pal, Lacey! This, I know, is gonna be a banner day. I let her snoop around some, then I go for her. Knock her out, strip her down, and do what I'd been wanting to do since I was a high school kid. Ah, she was fine, just fine. You oughta know, right? You haven't had a piece yet, you're missing a bet.

I don't kill her. No way. I've got big plans for her. So I leave. Only one car in the lot, that and a pickup truck. I knew the pickup belonged to the dog man, so the car has to be Lacey's. I get in, and lay down on the back floor.

It's a long wait. The cops come. I don't know, it's maybe an hour before she finally comes out. She checks the car real careful, almost like she knows I'm there. Doesn't see me, though. Course not. So she starts up the car and heads for home.

She lights up this cigarette, and I cough. God knows what she must've thought. Scared her plenty, though. Thinks I'm in the trunk, I guess. When she stops, she jumps on the trunk like maybe it isn't locked. Has her face pressed up against the back window and here I am, looking right at her with her cheek mashed in.

Then she runs off, goes in her house, and I get out of the car. I'm standing there, and out she comes with a revolver. Shit, this gal's got balls. She goes right to the trunk and opens it, planning to blast me to hell. Course, I'm not there. I'm over by her front door, now, waiting for her to come back and open it.

She gets it unlocked, and we're about to go in when this jock shows up. He's gonna play big hero and search around. So they go off together, and she doesn't bother to lock the door up, so I help myself and go inside.

Pretty soon, they come in. The guy looks all over the place. He wants to stay, but Lacey won't bite, so he runs off and she's finally alone.

Almost alone, right?

Gets herself some wine, and makes this call. That's how

I find out she works for the paper. Cute call. Doesn't tell what I did to her. That's gonna be her secret. Just between her and me. Like I say, you can't let a thing like that get around, not in a town like Oasis.

So after the call, lo and behold, she locks herself in the john and starts to run the bath. Never even suspects I'm right in there with her. I have myself a great time watching her strip, check herself out in the mirror, lay down in the tub, soap herself up, sip her wine. I just stand there enjoying it for a while. I figure, she's mine now. I own her. I can do what I want with her, as much as I want.

Well, I finally decide it's time to spook her, start showing her who's running the show. So I turn off the light. I hear her splashing. Then she's out of the tub and pointing this pistol at her door as if I'm gonna come bashing through it. I just stand behind her and enjoy it. She's scared shitless. I can hear her gasping, making little whiny sounds. I leave her alone till she starts to get dressed, then I nail her. This time's better than before. It's better when they're conscious, squirming and crying. Adds a little flavor to the proceedings, you know?

By the time I'm done, I'm beat. Busy day, right? So it's time to hit the sack. I tie her to the bed and blindfold her. Don't want her walking off – or limping, as the case may be. And I don't want her learning my little secret till I'm ready to spring it on her. I want to see her reaction.

Next morning, after some asshole comes to the door, I have another go at her. She's better than ever, squirming and fighting. That should've given me a clue: the bitch has a lot more guts than I counted on. But I figure, once she sees I'm invisible, she's gonna know she can't win. She'll fall in line.

I let her know my plan. She's gonna be like Robin in Iowa, gonna take care of me and keep her mouth shut, and go on about her business just like nothing'd happened. I warn her what'll happen if she screws up. Then I go ahead and untie her and take off the blindfold.

First thing she does, when she sees she can't see me, is

give me a kick in the nuts. Then she runs. But she's smart, gotta give her that. She doesn't try to run away, knows she can't get away from someone she can't see, so instead she goes in the kitchen thinking she'll finish me off. Throws flour on me so she can see where I am, and sticks a knife in my back.

That would've taken care of most guys, just like all the fuckin' bullets you pumped into me. But I'm not most guys, right? I've drunk at the river, all that shit. Got magic powers. So she hurts me and gets away, probably thinks she's killed me.

But she hasn't. I'm out of there and hiding by the time the cops show up. Well, I figure she'll come back sooner or later. I'll just wait her out.

That's what, Thursday? I hang around all day, and she doesn't come back. Then I hang around Friday. When she doesn't show up by Saturday, I figure it's gonna be a long wait if I don't get into action.

I know she works for the paper, right? So I figure somebody there's gonna know where to find her. Turns out, the cops are there. Somebody got offed with a letter opener, and there's a note makes it sound like I done it. Weird, huh? Anyway, I stick around till the cops go. There's only me and the editor. He's acting funny.

I get ready in case I have to follow him. Snatch a shirt and cowboy hat out of the cleaners next door. Hide the stuff out back, then I nail some bitch that's getting in her car. I park it near the *Trib*'s lot, check her purse to see she's got some blush-on for my face – better than nothing – and put my clothes in her car.

I'm all set, right? I just wait a while, and the editor shows up. He checks his car real careful. Good thing I didn't hide in it, huh?

So I follow him to Tucson, and the rest is history. You know the rest. Except maybe how I got in the room, that second time. Lowered myself on a sheet. Man, that was hairy!

When you got away that time, I figured I'd flush you out

with a fire. Used cleaning fluid. Started four fires, in all. Burned real good.

I would've had you and Lacey, only I got overconfident about the gun. Well, shit, can't win 'em all.

CHAPTER THIRTY-ONE

'MIGHT BE good for you to listen, Lacey.'

'Why?'

'Know your enemy,' Scott said.

She nodded. She wished she could leave and avoid the presence of Hoffman – even his voice disgusted and frightened her. But she was curious. 'I don't know,' she said.

'You'll have to hear him a lot,' he said, 'if you're going to collaborate on the book with me. Might as well get used to the idea.'

'Yeah. All right.'

Scott started the tape. 'Okay,' Hoffman said. 'You want me to talk, I'll talk.'

Dukane stepped over to a front window. He knelt at its side, and peered out.

Looking at Nancy? Wondering if he could save her?

'The one I really wanted, it was Lacey.'

She tried not to listen. She thought about Nancy.

The girl had been out there for nearly an hour now. Dukane had spent most of that time looking at her. 'She's gagged,' he'd told Lacey. That explained why there were no screams.

He'd discussed shooting at the ropes or stakes that pinioned her spread-eagled to the ground. But even if he could free her that way, he supposed a fusillade would tear her apart before she could make the door – particularly since she was bound fast to Jan's larger body. Maybe after dark . . .

The tape played on. Lacey found herself listening, appalled by the list of Hoffman's victims, by the bragging and insolent tone of his voice. She listened with dread to the ghastly method of transformation, sickened by the image of the severed head, the beans being pushed through its eyes, the drinking of blood. When he described his attack on Coral, she shivered at the memory of herself in the dark bathroom of her home.

His tale of perversion and slaughter went on and on. Lacey thought about going into the kitchen, standing by the sink, running the water full blast to drown out the hideous sound of his voice. But she couldn't force herself to leave. She felt compelled to listen, much as she might be drawn to a grisly accident, horrified and worried about the victims but curious to see their broken remains.

Scott flipped the cassette over.

Then Hoffman was in Oasis, looking for her name in the telephone directory. She remembered the series of obscene midnight calls that had made her life miserable two years ago until she took an unlisted number. Thank God for those calls. The new number had at least postponed Hoffman's attack. If she'd only stayed away from the market . . .

She gagged as Hoffman described eating the dog.

Then he was in the shower room at the high school, secretly touching the girls, following one home to rape her. Lacey knew most of the people in Oasis. She wondered who the girl was. Pitied her. But it could've been so much worse.

When he told of breaking his mother's fingers, Lacey knew what was coming. She didn't want to hear about the butcher job. With a finger in each ear, she blocked the sound. But her mind saw him hacking Elsie apart, wrapping the pieces in cellophane. Scott, sitting only a few feet away, looked at her with sadness in his eyes. Then he blushed and turned away.

Lacey took the fingers from her ears. 'Ah, she was fine,' Hoffman said. 'Just fine.' Who did he mean? 'You oughta know, right. You haven't had a piece yet, you're missing a bet.'

Scott glanced at her, made a shy smile, and lowered his gaze to the floor.

Lacey, suddenly understanding, felt heat rush to her skin. Bad enough that Hoffman should violate her, but to *brag* about it, to suggest that Scott . . . What could she expect from a bastard like Hoffman?

She listened to the way he hid in her car, how he sneaked into the house, how he stood close to her as she phoned James. With growing dread, she waited for his description of the attack. She watched Scott as Hoffman spoke. He sat with his legs crossed, his hands gripping his knees. 'This time's better than before. This time she's conscious, at least till the very end.' He stared at the floor, his face dark red. 'It's better when they're conscious, squirming and crying.' Scott raised his face. He looked at her, and she saw tears shining in his eyes.

My God, she thought, he's crying for me.

She hesitated only a moment, then crawled across the floor to him and sat at his side. He took her hand.

'First thing she does when she sees she can't see me, is give me a kick in the nuts.'

Scott squeezed her hand. He looked at her and grinned as Hoffman told how she stabbed him. Then they listened as he described following Carl to the hotel.

At last, it was over.

Scott turned off the machine.

Dukane turned away from the window, a strange pleased look on his face. He sat with his back to the wall. Grinning. 'Listening to him . . . I got an idea. I know how we might save Nancy. It's a risk for all of us. It may not even work, but it stands a decent chance. I think we owe it to her.'

'What's your idea?' Scott asked.

'Send Hoffman out for her.'

Lacey groaned as the words clutched her bowels. She felt numb all over.

'We'd have to let him loose,' Scott muttered.

'As I said, it's a risk. He might try to get away, or he might turn on us. In either case, he'd be hard to stop. But he's awfully worried about Laveda. I don't think he'd want to make a break, not with the place surrounded. By now, somebody out there might have a pair of those infra-red goggles.'

'The goggles could kill his chance of getting to Nancy.'

'We'd have surprise on our side. They probably aren't watching constantly with those things – if they have them at all. They certainly won't expect us to send Hoffman out for the girl.'

'I don't know.'

'Lacey?'

'I . . . He's a monster. He'll try something. He'll try to kill us or . . . if he does get away, all the innocent people he'll kill . . .'

'His chances of escape are remote,' said Dukane. 'I think he knows that. As long as he sticks with us, he has some firepower on his side. If I were him, I'd stick with us until I'm sure we've had it. *Then* I'd chance a break.'

'He's put Lacey through hell,' Scott said. 'If he does take you and me out . . . God only knows what he'd do to her.' He placed a hand on Lacey's knee, held it tightly. 'I don't want to risk that.'

'All right,' Dukane said.

'Wait.' Lacey covered Scott's hand and squeezed it. 'We can't leave her out there. She . . . as Matt said, we owe her. Let's give it a try.'

Lacey sat on the floor, her back to the couch, her legs drawn up protectively as Dukane led Hoffman in. One cuff was attached to Dukane's left wrist: the other stood out sideways.

Scott followed, several paces behind, with Jan's shotgun aimed toward the area above the floating cuff.

Lacey raised her revolver and aimed at the same empty space.

'If it ain't Annie Oakley,' Hoffman said. 'Don't look so worried, huh? I'm doing you guys a favor.'

As they approached the broken front window, Dukane

removed the handcuffs. He slid a small carving knife from his rear pocket. 'Take this,' he said. 'But leave it outside once you've cut her free.'

The knife left his hand. He backed away.

'I'm supposed to go out the window, right?'

'Right. We'll open the door on your way back.'

'*If* I come back, huh?'

'If you don't, you'll end up in Laveda's hands. Sooner or later.'

'Yeah yeah.'

'Get going.'

The knife, hovering several feet off the floor, turned toward the broken window. The end of its handle lowered against the sill.

'Holy fuckin' shit,' Hoffman said. He sounded impressed. 'Look at them, will you?'

'We've seen.'

'You just want the one underneath, right?'

'Right.'

'Other's dead as a carp.' The knife raised and shot through the opening. 'Ha! Right on target. She can't feel it anyway, huh?' After a pause, he said, 'Look out, belowwww.'

Dukane crouched by the window.

As Scott hurried to the other one, curiosity overcame Lacey's distaste. She joined him, pistol ready, and peered out. Immediately, she regretted it. She gagged, but managed to swallow the bitter fluid that gushed up her throat.

She forced herself not to look away. The arms and legs of both women were spread wide and bound to metal stakes, but the mangled carcass on top hid most of Nancy from her view. Flies swarmed over the tattered skin of Jan's back and rump. The rear of her head had been scraped bald. A splinter of bone protruded from her left arm. Her left leg was dislocated and stretched far longer than the other; Lacey saw a knife embedded in its buttock.

As she watched, the knife slid out. It moved slowly over the ground to the staked foot, and sawed through the rope.

Though Nancy's foot remained bound to Jan's, it was now free of the stake. It didn't move.

The knife crossed the area between the spread legs, and cut the next rope.

It dropped out of sight beside the legs, and reappeared sliding along the ground near Nancy's outstretched left arm. It cut through the rope, then returned over the ground to her side. It appeared again near the feet, crossed the space between them, and moved up the other side. It snaked the length of Nancy's right arm, sawed through the rope.

Dukane stepped to the door.

The women's feet wobbled slightly. Then they rose from the ground and the bodies jerked into motion. Gunfire broke the silence. Bullets kicked up dust around the dragging bodies. Dark matter burst from Jan's back. Her head jumped, pieces exploding away.

Dukane threw open the door.

The bodies bounced up the low stoop. More bullets smacked into Jan, splashing her like pebbles striking water.

Then they were inside. Dukane kicked the door shut. As slugs pounded through it, he lunged toward the raised feet of the women. The feet began to drop. He swung his pistol, but it swept through empty air. Scott raced to help. Dukane's head snapped sideways. He staggered and dropped to his knees. Scott clutched his own belly. As he doubled, his shirt collar and belt jerked taut. He was lifted high off the floor.

Lacey fired twice at the space beneath him.

Then he was slammed down. The tile floor pounded aside his hands and knees. His forehead hit with a thud.

Dukane shot over him. Four bullets hit the far wall, blasting holes in the plaster, knocking down a framed oil of a desert sunset. He came forward slowly, in a crouch, his head turning as if he thought he might see a target. The gun suddenly flew from his twisted hand. He grunted as the front of his pants dented in. His nose jerked sideways, spouting blood. Throwing himself forward, he reached out and fell.

Lacey fired above his back. Her bullet smacked the wall. She aimed over his head and fired again. His head jumped. For a sinking instant, she thought she'd hit Dukane. Then the head snapped down, thudding the floor. He went limp.

Lacey pushed herself to her feet. She stood with her back to the wall, pistol forward. Dukane and Scott both lay motionless on the red tile floor. She breathed hard. Her heart felt ready to explode.

'My turn,' Hoffman said.

From the left.

She shot at his voice. Splinters burst from the hall doorframe.

'Time for fun and games.'

She aimed again, then hesitated, realizing the six-shot pistol held only one more live cartridge. If she missed with this one . . .

She knew a target she couldn't miss.

With a quaking hand, she raised the pistol and pressed its muzzle to her head.

CHAPTER THIRTY-TWO

'GO ON,' said the voice in front of Lacey. 'I'll fuck you anyway. Only thing is, you won't get a chance to enjoy it.'

She tried to force her finger to move, to squeeze the stiff, curved metal of the trigger just a bit, just a quarter inch, just enough. But part of her mind resisted. She wanted to live. She gazed at Scott's unmoving body, and didn't want to leave him. She wanted to see him smile again, to hear his laughter, to feel his gentle arms around her. Even if only one more time. As she stared at Scott, he moved one hand slightly.

She thumbed back the pistol's hammer.

'*Adios*,' said Hoffman.

She stabbed the pistol forward, felt its muzzle stop against Hoffman, and jerked the trigger.

'Bitch!' he shrieked through the gun's roar.

Something clubbed her face, knocking her head back against the wall. Her hand stung. The pistol fell. Another blow struck her face. As she sagged, a hand clutched her throat. It held her to the wall. The neck of her tank top jerked out. The fabric stretched taut, popped, and tore down the front. Pain erupted in her breasts as he grabbed them and tugged her to the floor.

Her knees pounded the tile. He forced her backwards. Down beside Nancy. Beside Jan. She tried to raise her head, but had no strength. Warm fluid spilled onto her legs as the gym shorts were yanked down. Hoffman's blood! Her panties were ripped away.

Where's Scott? her mind screamed. *He's alive. She'd seen him move. Why doesn't he stop this!*

She gasped in agony as Hoffman shoved into her. He

rammed hard, one hand gripping her breast as if to keep her from being shoved over the floor by the force of his thrusts. A wetness splattered her shoulder as he plunged.

She should've . . . why hadn't she pulled the damn trigger on herself and ended it? Better that than . . .

He pushed her head sideways. As he chewed and sucked the side of her neck, she saw Jan's face inches away from her own. The blank, staring eyes. The flap of dark flesh hanging off her cheek. The torn lips baring her broken teeth.

Dead.

Better this. Hoffman grunting and slobbering, twisting her skin, battering her insides with his vile organ. Better this than like Jan.

She lowered her gaze to the wide, blinking eyes of Nancy. They were filled with terror, but alive.

Where's Scott!

Hoffman's weight was on her now, crushing her chest, his mouth mashing her lips, suffocating her as he pounded down with his pelvis. Then he was rigid. Lacey felt his jerking throb inside her, the spurt of fluid.

He lay on top of her, breathing heavily. At last, his weight lifted. She felt his organ slide out.

She raised her head enough to see Scott and Dukane still unconscious on the floor.

'Guess what's next,' Hoffman hissed.

Lacey shut her eyes and said nothing.

He grabbed her hair and pulled her to her feet. 'One guess, cunt.' He paused. 'No? Well, just watch and see.'

The door flew open behind Lacey. A hand squeezed the back of her neck. Another clutched between her legs. She was lifted off her feet and hurled outside.

She hit the ground hard, tumbling, gasping as gravel and cactus tore her skin. Then she lay still and awaited the hail of bullets.

CHAPTER THIRTY-THREE

DUKANE'S HEAD throbbed with fire. He lay motionless, feeling the floor under him, wondering what had happened. Slowly, he remembered. Guilt hit him like a club.

What have I done!

He forced himself to open one eye. The living room was bright with sunlight. Nearby was the sprawled body of Scott, hands cuffed behind him.

Dukane was tied with electrical cord. As he struggled to free himself, he heard a quiet sob.

'Scott?' he whispered.

The body rolled over. 'Matt?' His face was wet with tears. 'I thought you were dead.'

'Where's Hoffman?'

'I . . . I don't know. He took Nancy into the bedroom a few minutes ago. Probably in there. Matt, Lacey's . . .' He choked back a sob. 'Lacey's gone.'

'Where?'

Scott shook his head. 'I came to . . . asked Hoffman. He just laughed.'

'Shit.'

'Oh God, Matt . . .'

'Take it easy.' He jerked his hands free. Grimacing as pain cut into his head like a lance, he rolled onto his side and untied the knotted cord at his feet. He scanned the room, and flinched. In the rocking chair facing the broken front window sat Jan. The shotgun rested over the sill, aiming outside.

'Beau Geste,' Scott muttered.

'Maybe the shotgun's loaded.' Dukane forced himself to stand. He took one step.

A tinny, amplified voice said, 'We want Hoffman. You've got five minutes. Bring him out, and we'll let you go. If not, you'll all die. The girl first.'

'Lacey,' Scott whispered.

Dukane rushed to the window. As he reached for the shotgun, he looked out.

He saw Lacey. A hundred yards away. Sprawled across the hood of the Rolls Royce. Her arms and legs were outstretched and tied.

A dozen men and women stood near the car, watching as a woman lashed her once with a thin, golden chain.

The woman was naked. Glossy, blonde hair draped her back. Her gold arm bands glinted sunlight.

Laveda!

In spite of the heat, gooseflesh prickled Dukane's skin.

Lacey's quiet gasp of pain came through the silence as the chain struck again.

Dukane grabbed the double-barreled shotgun. He broke it open. The chambers were empty. Turning from the window, he looked for other weapons. The pistols were nowhere in sight. He quietly closed the breach.

'Four minutes,' the distant voice announced.

Dukane hurried to Scott. He fished a key from his pocket and knelt to unlock the cuffs.

'Is it Lacey?'

'Yes.'

'Oh God.'

'Come on.' Dukane tiptoed into the hallway, Scott close behind him. The bathroom door stood open. The bedroom door was shut. Almost.

He stepped quietly toward it. Stopped.

From inside came muffled grunting sounds, the creak of bedsprings.

Nancy lay on the bed, her sweat-slick body pounding against the mattress, arms stretched overhead, breasts oddly mashed, legs wide open and twitching, the lips of her vagina spread far apart like an open, sucking mouth. Dukane heard the slap of flesh, and wet, smacking sounds.

'Three minutes,' announced the amplified voice.

Dukane shouldered open the door. He ran for the bed, reversing the shotgun, raising it high by its barrels.

Nancy's wet eyes looked up at him. She turned her head away as he swung the shotgun down.

It stopped before hitting her, stopped six inches above her face, stopped with a crashing thud like a coconut hurled against concrete. The stock of the shotgun split on impact. Teethmarks appeared in Nancy's cheek – empty, ragged holes that quickly filled with blood.

Scott dived onto her. He groped above her left arm, grabbed, snapped a handcuff in place, closed the other bracelet around his own wrist.

'Got him!' Scott cried.

CHAPTER THIRTY-FOUR

'YOU HAVE two minutes,' said the man with the megaphone.

Even as he spoke, the thin chain twirled over the head of the woman beside Lacey, its gold links flashing sunlight, and whistled down. She cried out as it cut fire across her breasts. A smile trembled on the woman's lips. Her nipples stood erect on her sweaty breasts.

She's getting off, Lacey thought.

It must've been at her command that the rifles hadn't opened up on Lacey, that instead the Rolls had come for her. She'd watched it approach, too frightened to move, thinking *it's dead*, Dukane got it with a Molotov cocktail, how can it be coming? It bore down on her, its grill blinding in the sunlight. She thought it might crush her into the gravel, but it slipped sideways and its black front tire missed by inches. A door flew open. She was dragged inside the chilly, air-conditioned car.

Two men held her across their laps, pawing her as the car sped away.

The chain whipped down, lashing her belly.

The woman was breathing hard. But not from the exertion. She licked her lips, and struck again. Lacey jerked rigid as the chain cut her thighs.

It was the woman who ordered her tied to the car's hood. The sun-baked metal had scorched her, but the pain of the burnt flesh faded when the whipping started.

The chain whished down, biting into her shoulder and breast.

A man suddenly threw himself onto her, licking the blood from her breast.

The woman lashed him. 'Not yet!' she snapped.

Others jerked him away.

'One minute,' said the man with the megaphone.

'They won't come,' said a stocky, red-faced man.

The chain slashed her belly.

'I did not expect them to come,' the woman said in a trembling voice. 'They threw her out. She's ours.'

'Will we drink?' asked a voice.

'When I am done with her.' Again, the chain whipped down.

Lacey bucked as it tore her.

'The dagger.'

A teenaged girl in a bikini and Dodger cap handed a knife to her. Lacey stared at its thin, tapering blade.

'The river flows,' said the woman.

'The river is red,' chanted the others.

'The river flows!'

'Flows from the heart.'

'The river . . .'

'They're coming out!' a man cried.

Lifting her head, Lacey stared over her torn body. Dukane and Scott were out of the house, walking slowly forward, tugging at the open space between them.

She glanced at the woman, saw a fierce smile on her face.

'Tell the snipers not to shoot. I want all three alive.'

A man spoke over his megaphone, ordering everyone to hold fire.

On both sides of the car, men and women lowered their weapons.

Lacey gazed at Scott, watched him struggle to hold his invisible, silent captive. The pain of her wounds was forgotten as gratitude and despair brought tears to her eyes.

They're doing this for me, she realized.

Sacrificing themselves.

If only she'd had the courage to end her life back at the house when she had the chance . . .

They were thirty yards away.

'Go back!' she yelled, but she knew it was too late.

The men kept coming, jerking and swaying as if the beast between them fought to free himself.

Twenty yards.

She could see the grim, determined look on Scott's face.

Ten yards.

A low laugh came from the woman. 'Bring him to me,' she called. 'I have waited a long time for Samuel Hoffman. And for you, Matthew Dukane. This will be a great day for me.'

'Every dog has its day,' Dukane said. One side of his mouth curled into a smile.

He and Scott sprang apart, diving sideways and rolling through the dust. Four pistols appeared from behind them. They stopped rolling, and their gunfire stuttered through the stillness in a deafening roar.

Bodies whirled and flopped. Dirt exploded around Scott and Dukane as their fire was returned. Screams tore through the din. A man clutched his belly and sat down hard. The ball cap and bloody matter flew from the head of the teenaged girl as she fired at Dukane. He tossed a pistol aside and kept firing his automatic. A man spun, crashed into the side of the car, and fell.

Dukane yelled as he was hit.

Scott rose to one knee, not even glancing at him, shoving a fresh magazine into the handle of his .45. Gravel kicked up beside his foot, but he didn't flinch. He worked the slide and resumed firing.

Dukane was on his knees, his left arm hanging limp firing with his right.

A man raced forward, shooting. A bullet slammed him down.

Abruptly, there was silence.

Jerking her head from side to side, Lacey saw no one still standing. On both sides of the car lay crumpled bodies

Scott ran forward in a crouch. Far off, a rifle cracked Dirt spouted in front of him.

As Dukane dropped and crawled forward, Scott dived to the ground near a fat man. He grabbed the man's rifle. It had a telescopic sight. Settling himself in a prone position, he aimed toward the far left of the house.

A distant shot. The top of a cactus near Dukane exploded. Scott fired, then made a thumbs-up sign at Dukane. He swung the barrel to his right.

Dukane scurried forward. He reached the front of the car, and began to cut the rope at Lacey's foot.

A shot thunked the grill.

Scott fired. 'Watch it,' he called. 'Still one out there.'

Dukane freed Lacey's left hand, then rushed around the rear of the car and came up at her other side. As he sliced through the rope, a shot rang out. The bullet smacked the windshield inches above her head.

He scurried to the front.

Scott fired. 'Got him!' he yelled. 'That oughta be it.'

Lacey sat up. As soon as her right foot was loose, she scooted off the hood. Scott, hurrying toward her, passed the rifle to Dukane and pulled off his shirt. He draped the shirt over Lacey's back. Holding her by the shoulders, he looked down at her torn body. 'Oh God, Lacey,' he murmured. 'I'm sorry. I'm so sorry.'

With blurry, tear-filled eyes, she stared at his tormented face. She kissed him. Then she managed a smile. 'Who do you think you are, James Bond?'

'Max Carter and Charlie Dane.'

Dukane came up behind him. 'I think I deserve a kiss, too.'

He got one. Lacey hugged him, ignoring the pain of her own wounds, and kissed his dry lips.

'You guys are nuts, coming out like that.'

'The best defense . . .' Dukane said.

Lacey gasped, her joy suddenly turning to cold fear. Hoffman! You let him . . .' She staggered back, clutching the shirt tight to hide her nakedness, looking behind her as if she might somehow see him sneaking up.

'Hoffman isn't with us,' Dukane said.

'I know. You let him . . .'

'He's still in the house,' Scott interrupted. 'Securely handcuffed in the bathroom.'

'You mean . . .?'

'Pretty good act, huh?'

'Now,' said Dukane, 'how about attending to my arm before I bleed to death?'

'Oh,' Scott muttered. 'Forgot about that.'

'I didn't.'

CHAPTER THIRTY-FIVE

THE BULLET had smashed a bone in Dukane's forearm. Scott broke the stock off a rifle, and made ungainly splints from it. He used strips of Dukane's shirt to bandage the wound and lash the splints into place.

'We'd better get you to a hospital,' he said. 'Both of you, and Nancy.'

'All in good time. See if the car works.'

Scott helped Lacey inside.

'Right with you,' Dukane said.

As Scott climbed into the driver's seat, Dukane wandered from body to body, crouching over several of the women for a closer inspection.

Scott turned the ignition key. The car came to life, blowing cool, welcome air onto Lacey.

'What's he looking for?' she asked.

Scott shook his head.

Finally, Dukane climbed into the back seat. In each hand, he held a large gold band, the bands Lacey had seen on the arms of the woman who'd whipped her. 'I know I hit the bitch,' he said. 'Saw her go down.'

'Who?'

'Laveda. But she's not here now. Just her damn jewelry. Did you see anyone run off?'

'No,' Scott said. 'I thought we got them all.'

'Okay. Let's pick up Hoffman and Nancy, and get the hell out of here.'

The car sped forward, bumping over the rough earth, down a gradual slope, and up a rise to the flat area in front of the house. Scott turned off the engine. 'You can wait here if you want,' he told Lacey.

211

She didn't want to be left alone. 'I'll go in,' she said.

Scott pulled the key from the ignition and stepped out. Lacey opened her door. Stifling heat wrapped her like a blanket as she climbed out. She glimpsed the body of the man under the broken window, hammer still clutched in his outflung hand.

She entered the house behind Scott. Dukane followed and shut the door. The house was silent.

'Nancy?' Dukane called.

No answer.

He suddenly broke into a run, vanishing down the hall. Scott and Lacey rushed after him.

The bedroom was empty.

'Nancy?'

From the closet came a muffled sob.

Dukane jerked its door open.

Nancy sat crouched in a corner, half hidden behind hanging dresses. Her black hair clung to her face with sweat. Though the room was hot and she wore jeans and a wool shirt, Lacey could see her shivering.

'It's all right,' Dukane told her. 'It's over. Everything's fine.'

'No,' she gasped, batting away his hands as he reached for her. Her wide eyes blinked. 'Not over. Wanta hide.'

From behind them came a scream that washed over Lacey like a vile, chilling flood. It was the scream of a man.

'Get Nancy out of here,' Scott snapped, and ran after Dukane.

Lacey dropped to her knees. She tried to grab the girl's flailing hands. 'Stop!' she cried. Then she clutched a foot and dragged Nancy from the closet. She pulled the girl to her feet, tugged her into the hall.

From there, she saw Dukane slam the bathroom door, shutting himself and Scott inside.

Screams filled her ears as she led Nancy through the living room. 'Wait in the car,' she said.

Then she raced to the hall.

The bathroom door flew open. Dukane staggered backwards through it, and fell. The wooden hilt of a butcher knife stood upright in his belly.

As she ran toward him, she heard a *whup* like the sound of a wind-flapped canvas. Fire exploded through the doorway.

'Scott!' she shrieked.

The fire lapped her body, forcing her away from the door. She shielded her eyes and gazed into the inferno. Near the floor, she saw a hole in the fire as if a tunnel had been dug in the flames – a writhing tunnel shaped like a man.

A passage opened in the blaze. It rushed toward her. Smashed her aside. She tripped over Dukane. As she slammed the far wall, she saw a flaming figure race down the hallway, arms waving, hair ablaze.

Scott? She ran after it. As it lurched across the living room, she realized she could see through it: the fire blazed around a hollow shell. It fell against a window. The curtains caught fire. As it lurched out the front door, it turned and Lacey glimpsed its fire-wrapped face, its breasts.

She rushed back to the bathroom.

'Scott!' she cried out. '*Scott!*'

The wall of fire roared.

CHAPTER THIRTY-SIX

LACEY CIRCLED the block twice, watching for strangers, then killed the headlights and steered the Firebird up the narrow driveway to her garage. She put it into the garage, and entered her house by the back door.

The lights were off. She left them that way.

Searching the dark house, she remembered how she and Cliff had gone through it that night so long ago – only a few days ago. They'd found no one then. Lacey found no one now. But she couldn't be certain she was alone: she could never be sure of that again.

Though filthy, she was afraid to use her tub.

Though dazed and weary, she was afraid to use her bed.

She arranged blankets inside her walk-in closet, and lay down there. It reminded her of the nest in the hallway that she'd shared with Scott.

Thoughts of Scott swirled through her mind as she tried to sleep. Other thoughts, too. Bad ones that made her shake.

Three times during the night, she heard sounds in the house that made her sweat and hold her breath. Afraid to investigate, she lay there rigid until exhaustion forced her to fall limp and gasp for air.

Once, as she drifted off, the closet door swung silently open. The dark figure of a man knelt over her. She quaked with terror until he spoke.

'It's just me,' he said.

'Scott?'

'I had a hard time finding you. What're you hiding from?'

'Everything.'

'Don't be afraid.'

'Oh Scott, I thought you were dead.'

Then he came down and kissed her, and his charred lips crumbled and filled her mouth with ashes.

She bolted upright, gasping, and found herself alone in the closet. Its door was still shut.

After a moment's hesitation, she pushed open the door. She studied the familiar, night shadows of her bedroom, then crawled over the carpet to the alarm clock. Four-thirty.

Time to begin.

Lacey tiptoed through the dark silence of the house. She searched cupboards in the kitchen, found what she wanted, and stepped outside.

She entered her garage through a side door connecting it to the laundry room. A dim light went on inside the Firebird when she opened its door. Kneeling on the passenger seat, she reached out and drew its keys from the ignition.

The Firebird was one of the four cars she'd found after she ran from the burning house and discovered the keys of the Rolls Royce were gone. She and Nancy had dashed up the long entry road, and come upon the cars of the dead people. She'd insisted Nancy take one of them, and leave her.

Now, keys in hand, Lacey crawled out of the Firebird. She left its door open for light, and walked over the warm concrete to the trunk. Taking a deep breath, she unlocked it. The lid swung up.

As dawn lightened the sky, Lacey twisted off the plastic cap. She raised the bottle to her lips. Its strong fumes made her throat clutch, but she filled her mouth anyway to wash out the other taste – the sour taste of the vomit that had flooded out after the blood.

She spat the brandy onto the loose earth at her feet, then upended the bottle. The amber fluid gurgled out, splashing onto the dirt.

When it was empty, she tossed it aside. It fell to the grass beside the cellophane package of beans and the knife.

She put her clothes back on, covering her blood-spattered nakedness.

Then she picked up her shovel. She set it inside the laundry room. Shutting the door, she started for her house.

A man stepped around the corner.

Numb with fear, she staggered back.

The man didn't move.

She gazed at him, at his blackened face and torso, his hairless scalp, his scorched and tattered pants – and recognized the phantom from her nightmares. She pressed trembling hands to her eyes. At the sound of footsteps, she lowered them.

He was walking toward her, his sooty hands reaching out.

'Thought you'd be glad to see me,' he said. 'I know I look like a wreck, but . . .'

'Scott,' she muttered.

He clutched her shoulders and drew her against his body. His cracked, dry lips pressed her mouth. She felt the wetness of his tongue. His hands stroked her hair, the sides of her face.

'It *is* you?' she whispered. Scott's grimy, grinning face blurred as tears filled Lacey's eyes.

CHAPTER THIRTY-SEVEN

HE GUZZLED half a bottle of Bud, leaned back on the kitchen chair, and sighed.

'That was Hoffman we heard screaming. When Matt and I ran in the bathroom, all we saw was this butcher knife jerking around right above the floor. And the handcuffs shaking. Laveda must've made herself invisible when the shooting started. Must've had a bean left over from the time she'd gone through the process a year ago.

'She went for Matt. That gave me a chance to douse her with gas and touch her off. The whole gas can went up, though. I thought I was cooked, but I dived out the bathroom window. The fall . . . it knocked me out cold. Don't think I was out for long, but by the time I reached the front of the house, I saw you and Nancy running off.'

'Why didn't you yell?'

He shook his head and took another gulp of beer. 'I figured I could catch up later. The main thing was to get Matt out of the house.'

'You went back in?'

'Had to. Couldn't leave him in there. I got to him just before the fire did, dragged him out, patched up his stomach wound the best I could, and threw him into the car. When I drove up the road, you and Nancy were nowhere in sight. I figured you'd be all right, though, so I drove like hell back to Tucson and got him into an emergency room. I didn't think he'd make it, but he's a tough son of a bitch. They had him in stable condition by the time I left.'

'He's *alive*?' Lacey grinned. 'Well. What do you know?'

'When I got back to the house and couldn't find you, I suspected you might come back here.'

'I didn't know where else to go.'

'Not the greatest hide-out in the world.'

'I had a plan,' she admitted, and lowered her eyes. Until now, the plan had seemed like her only chance for survival. With Scott sitting across the breakfast table, it seemed ridiculous and perverse. She didn't want to tell him about it.

'In your place,' Scott said, 'I might've tried the same thing.'

'You know?'

'I saw the empty brandy bottle out back. And the sack of beans. And where you dug the hole.'

'The . . . the rest of the body's still in the garage. I found her . . . near where they'd left their cars. After I sent Nancy away, I . . . a bean was in the dirt by her mouth. That's what gave me the idea. If I were invisible, nobody could get me. I tried the bean, but it didn't make me invisible. So then I put her body in the trunk of a car and . . . God, it was all burnt and crumbly and . . .'

'It was Laveda!'

Lacey nodded. 'I guess so.'

Reaching out, Scott squeezed her hand. 'Then it's over.'

That night, he dug up the head. They drove far out in the desert, and poured gasoline over the remains of Laveda. The fire burned for a long time. When it finally dwindled, they dug two holes in the sand and buried the smoldering head a great distance from the body.

RICHARD LAYMON

ALLHALLOWS EVE

A standard well-fitted-out bathroom: tiles, towelling rugs on the floor, towels on heated rails, mirrored medicine cabinet above the basin, a laundry basket in one corner and the usual litter of plastic bottles and aerosols.

Rubbing the fatigue out of his eyes, he lifted the toilet seat. And saw the water, pink-tinged, saw the head staring up at him with empty eye-sockets, the grey hair floating, shifting as though troubled by a slow current.

Retching and gagging, his hand clamped desperately over his mouth, he lurched across to the shower curtain, ripped it aside and doubled up over the bath. And saw the naked torso, the arms and legs severed and laid out neatly round it as though for some grotesque kit inspection . . .

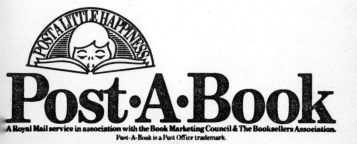

POST A LITTLE HAPPINESS

Post·A·Book

A Royal Mail service in association with the Book Marketing Council & The Booksellers Association.

Post-A-Book is a Post Office trademark.

DOUGLAS CLEGG

GOAT DANCE

It begins with a dream of buried children.

It begins with human sacrifice.

It begins with the need for new blood.

Malcolm Coffey thought he had buried his past, but it had scraped its way out of its grave. His past was tracking him down, dragging its flayed body, surrounded by its ravenous minions, towards him, worming its blood-hungry passage into his mind, into his body . . .

There is a place where nightmares begin.

There is a town where night never ends.

There is a breeding ground for horror. The horror called the Goat Dance.

HODDER AND STOUGHTON PAPERBACKS

JOHN FARRIS

SCARE TACTICS

An experience in total terror that will bind you and carry you helplessly back to the supernatural sorcery of ancient Babylon, to the awful spectacle of reincarnated gods, the mysteries of life after death and the horrendous power of forces from beyond the grave . . .

Scare Tactics brings together five mind-freezing examples of John Farris' psychopathic imagination. Welcome to his world – but enter with care.

'One of the giants of contemporary horror' *Peter Straub*

'John Farris has a genius for creating compelling suspense' *Peter Benchley*

HODDER AND STOUGHTON PAPERBACKS

MORE HORROR TITLES AVAILABLE FROM
HODDER AND STOUGHTON PAPERBACKS

DOUGLAS CLEGG

	52255 5	Goat Dance	£3.99
	55115 6	Breeder	£3.99
	56228 X	Neverland	£4.99

JOHN FARRIS

	52254 7	Scare Tactics	£3.50
	40575 3	Son of the Endless Night	£4.99
	53717 X	The Axeman Cometh	£3.50

JOE LANSDALE

| | 51570 2 | The Drive-In | £2.99 |
| | 53219 4 | The Drive-In 2 | £2.99 |

RICHARD LAYMON

	05803 4	Allhallows Eve	£4.50
	39353 4	Beasthouse	£4.99
	05706 2	Night Show	£4.50

All these books are available at your local bookshop or newsagent, or can be ordered direct from the publisher. Just tick the titles you want and fill in the form below.

Prices and availability subject to change without notice.

HODDER AND STOUGHTON PAPERBACKS, P.O. Box 11, Falmouth, Cornwall.

Please send cheque or postal order for the value of the book, and add the following for postage and packing:

UK including BFPO – £1.00 for one book, plus 50p for the second book, and 30p for each additional book ordered up to a £3.00 maximum.

OVERSEAS INCLUDING EIRE – £2.00 for the first book, plus £1.00 for the second book, and 50p for each additional book ordered.
OR Please debit this amount from my Access/Visa Card (delete as appropriate).

CARD NUMBER ☐☐☐☐☐☐☐☐☐☐☐☐☐☐☐☐☐☐

AMOUNT £...

EXPIRY DATE..

SIGNED..

NAME...

ADDRESS..